3 Boons Give and Take

3 Boons Give and Take

B. Manjula Rao

PARTRIDGE

ISBN: Hardcover   978-1-4828-7485-3
             Softcover   978-1-4828-7484-6
             eBook   978-1-4828-7483-9

Print information available on the last page.

To order additional copies of this book, contact
Partridge India
000 800 10062 62
orders.india@partridgepublishing.com

www.partridgepublishing.com/india

'Let the divine inspire us . . .'

PROLOGUE

The magnificent universe created by God is filled with people of various walks of life located sometimes in a village, which seems to have come out alive from a beautiful postcard, or in a city with huge opportunity, which holds the imagination of every youngster. 'Almighty has created each one of us for a reason,' they say. Born for a purpose, we wander aimlessly until one day we become aware of it.

To the Hon'ble Prime Minister Sri. Narendra Modiji for his brilliant initiative '*Swachh Bharat Abhiyan*'.

CHAPTER ONE

It was a bright October morning, just another day in Mumbai. Sid got up and made coffee for himself. He sipped his coffee slowly and noticed the time.

Normally, he would start off early to avoid the ever-increasing Mumbai traffic. Damn it! He was late. He took a quick shower. He stuffed the laptop cable hurriedly into the laptop bag. The well-known October heat in Mumbai had kept him awake the whole night. The reason was, well, his air conditioner had conked out. He had been busy the entire week to get it repaired.

I must call the technician today, he thought.

Gulping down the leftover coffee from the cup, he took his car key and left for his office quickly – a typical morning in Sid's life.

Here was Siddarth Malhotra or Sid as he was known living in our very own universe. He was an exceptionally handsome, tall Punjabi boy and an investment banker by profession. He had climbed up the corporate ladder at a very young age. He was popular not only for his dashing personality but also for his aggressiveness at work. Young interns who would join the company to gain some experience would be thrilled when they were put under his charge. Seemingly so, Sid was a go-getter who had joined the Ascii (97–122) Solutions workforce as an investment banking analyst and had reached the position of a vice-president at the age of thirty-three by sheer hard work and dedication. He was loved by his team, and his boss had a high opinion of him.

Being the only child of his parents, who resided in Chandigarh, Sid had a comfortable and loving upbringing. His father worked for a nationalised bank and retired as a general manager. His father's work took him to different places, so Sid grew up in various places, changing schools often and learning different languages. His father was a man of few words, and his mother like every mother fussed about him a little too much, which made him want to spend most of his time with his grandpa.

While growing up, his grandpa was his constant companion. He would come over during Sid's vacation and spend time with him. It was a ritual that he never broke. He shared his bedroom along with his deepest secrets with his grandpa. Be it his pranks as a child or his crushes as a teenager, his grandpa knew them all.

During holidays, he would accompany him for long walks. They would talk about his school and friends. He was all ears to any problem Sid had. He would share his experiences as a child, which amused Sid.

His grandpa grew up in Burma, now Myanmar. His father was the first allopath doctor in his town. He served the British. He was posted to Burma on an assignment by the British. He would relate how as a child the only mode of transport was an elephant. They travelled far and wide, healing people who suffered from various ailments.

As a child, his grandpa was diagnosed with acute stomach ulcer. The pain was so bad that he could not digest anything other than bread, which he happened to eat by chance at one of his friend's home. Those days, bread was a new form of diet, which a few rich could afford. They had to barter for the same. A kilo of rice would fetch them a loaf of bread. But his parents did not complain. They were willing to do anything for their only child.

Electricity was unheard of, and they lived in complete isolation. Communication was unbelievable. There was a time when his aunt's daughter was to be married, they received the invite almost a year later.

These stories had a profound impact on Sid's life later.

Sid was academically bright with good values instilled upon him by his parents and grandpa. He got into Electronics branch of Engineering in Delhi. The four years there were uneventful and flew by in no time. He shared his room with Partiv Singh.

Partiv was a son of a garment shop owner. His family was into cloth business for generations. They owned a shop at the bustling marketplace of Chandini Chowk in Delhi. He was the first one from the family to get into engineering.

He was introduced as, '*Yeh hamara pada likha bacha.*'

His parents were extremely supportive. He had three elder sisters, out of which the eldest was married. There were talks of marriage of the second one. They lived in an ancestral home, which was as chaotic as the people in it. It was a huge joint family with sixteen members in all. It was built and rebuilt time and again to suit the needs of people who lived there. This made it look more like a home that had just been hit by a tsunami. Partiv hated the place but did not express his opinion though. The constant chatter, petty fights, the noise, and everything about it were nauseating. So when he got into the engineering college, the first thing that made him extremely happy was that he was to stay in a hostel. Initially, the family did not like the idea.

'None of our family members have ever stayed in a hostel,' said his *Thavuji*.

'But *Bhaiya* none of our family members have studied beyond grade 10,' said Partiv's father.

'He is the first one to be an engineer in our family,' added one of his cousins who was glad that if Partiv left, he would have the room for himself.

'I know that. But why stay in a hostel when you can travel from home?' asked *Thavuji*.

How could anyone call this zoo a home? Partiv wondered.

'I don't want to go either, but that is not important. There are classes in the evening, and it would be a little unsafe to travel back home in the night,' said Partiv softly with little interest.

He knew his *Thavuji* well.

'Look at him, he looks so unhappy,' said his *Thavuji*.

Finally, they agreed, and the following day, he filled the form for hostel facility.

He was very happy in the hostel. At least he had a bed and peace here. He stayed there even during the holidays. When asked, he would simply say he had project work to be completed. He liked Sid and spent most of his time with him. In his final year, he got specialised in Artificial Intelligence. Having a huge scope in abroad, he got a job in an automobile company in the United States. Within a matter of months, they parted ways promising to keep in touch. Partiv went abroad, and Sid took up management studies.

Why management? Well! That was a big question. It was never follow your heart it was like follow the crowd. Better the business school, the easier it was to break into the investment banking industry. This was one of the coveted jobs as there was big money. It was soon becoming one of the vibrant segments of financial services where every MBA student dreamt of being placed. They relied heavily on campus recruitments. Sid looked forward to being placed too.

During his final year, Sid attended many campus interviews, which tested his knowledge of financial and business concepts, interpersonal and negotiation skills.

One of the companies that interested him the most was Ascii (97–122) Solutions based in Mumbai. They provided financial solutions for their clients across the industries. They helped public and private corporations in levitating funds and providing strategic advisory services for expansion, acquisitions, and mergers. They worked on two main areas – investment banking and the financing group. This was one company that seemed to be open to new ideas and was keen on hearing him. When he was asked which division of banking interested him the most, **Sid** said, without contemplating too much, 'Mergers and acquisitions.'

Soon, what followed was a ten-minute talk on how he would love to give advice to the buyers and sellers on business assessment, negotiation, pricing, and shaping of transactions and also how good he was at its implementation.

He was asked many more questions on how he would be helping clients solve some of their most critical financial and strategic challenges. Sid answered most of them to the best of his abilities. There were a few more queries where his knowledge on international business scenario and regulatory bodies were put to test. Sid did just fine in those areas.

He got employed at Ascii (97–122) Solutions in Mumbai as an analyst in M&A. It was a defining moment for Sid. Yes, this was his first job. Most of his batchmates were placed in different parts of the country. They partied hard that night.

He was to move to Mumbai soon. This made his parents a little anxious. He suggested that they could live with him. After giving it a thought, the Malhotras dismissed the idea as they found Chandigarh an ideal place to spend their retired life in slow pace.

A few months later, Sid set out to Mumbai, a city he had visited once earlier for a distant cousin's wedding. The city was, as usual, bustling with activity. It had changed over a period of time. There were new constructions and more people. This was a story of every metro these days.

He walked out of the arrivals of terminal 1B Mumbai airport. He saw a huge placard with his name written over it boldly. It was the hotel personnel. He made his way towards it. Soon, he was checked into the hotel.

The following morning, he reported to his place of work at Bandra Kurla Complex exactly at 9 a.m. The office was on the fourth floor. He walked into the reception and gave his name. He was asked to wait. He sat down looking around. Soon, a man named Mr Jayesh came over and introduced himself and showed him around. He was introduced to the other staff members. It was a quick 'hello', and they were back to work.

In a few days, Sid got settled down in the new place. He soon moved in with a colleague Aman Sood. He worked as an associate and was with the company for past three years. He was looking for someone to share the flat, which was located in the suburbs of Mumbai, Bandra. It was an expensive locality. Though it was a small house consisting of kitchen, hall, and a bedroom, it was spacious compared to Mumbai standards. Sid made himself comfortable in the hall. The place was close to his office and hence convenient.

The office atmosphere was pleasant but highly competitive. He attended a training programme with a bunch of other analysts for a week. They were trained on various fronts including product specialisation and financial models. As there was huge development in the field of information technology in recent times, complicated tools for decision-making and in-depth valuation were made available, which would help them manage and annunciate client's data in negligible time.

The workload as an analyst was immense. He took care of all the administration work necessary in the process of making a deal. It was 24/7 kind of job with most of the business being done over the phone.

He had to valuate a company and then sell it to a prospective client. Sometimes, he felt like a fortune-teller. There was the usual office politics and romances like who was bootlicking his senior or who was going out with his junior blah . . . blah . . .

Sid tried not to get involved. He turned a blind eye even to the most salacious gossip. In case of an argument, he remained as neutral as possible without offending anyone. Diplomacy was essential for survival.

As most of his clients were abroad, the time difference took a toll. During the daytime, he would be working his ass off in the office, and once home, he would hardly have time for a quick shower and dinner, and then he would be back on conference calls.

Sid was a fitness freak. However busy the schedule would be, he would take some time for a twenty-minute session of cardio.

He hated the paperwork and the presentations. The only thing that kept him going was that the banking industry was a people-based business and Sid loved interacting with people. He had categorised his clients into three categories: science, commerce, and humanities. Of course, this had nothing to do with their qualifications; it was more of their personality. The first category spoke less and was good listeners. They believed in a greater good. The second category was the ones who wanted every penny they invested in doubled and in a short period of time and hell bent on teaching him how to do his job. The third category hardly interfered. They let Sid handle their investment completely.

Though it took some time to earn those big numbers, he had already designed a career chart. He had designated a goal for himself and took keen interest in what was going around him.

The opportunity to learn something new had his adrenaline soaring. His belief was to achieve great things in short time. His routine was a cycle of home-office-home. Having come to a city with no friends or relatives, he spent most of his time, even the weekends, working.

After a few months, Aman Sood got a better opportunity in Noida. Initially, he was a little unsure, but later, he decided to take the offer. Noida was close to his hometown Delhi, where his parents lived. Within three months, Aman vacated the flat. Having no choice, Sid rented out the flat for himself.

Sid felt a little empty for few days as he was quite close to Aman. But then it was business, as usual. Back in Ascii (97–122) Solutions, his place was taken by Rishabh Patil.

Rishabh was a man of few words and a complete gentleman. He was a couple of years younger than Sid. He was short, average-looking, and healthier. He mostly kept to himself. He was a Gujarati and married for over a year now. He was a typical Mumbaitie from suburbs of Mumbai, Vileparle. This area was populated by the Gujarati community, hence known for Gujaratis run colleges and food joints. Rishabh lived with his parents. Earlier, Rishabh was engaged to Falguni Shah, who lived a few blocks away. They had known each other since childhood. They had gone to the same school and graduated from the same college. Their relationship was known to their respective parents, and they had approved of it.

On the day of their graduation results, Rishabh picked up Falguni from her home. As soon as they reached the college compound, Rishabh dropped Falguni and went in search of parking place for his two-wheeler.

Falguni spotted two of her friends on the other side of the road and walked towards them in excitement. As she was crossing the road, a car appeared suddenly from nowhere and ran over her recklessly, leaving Falguni in a pool of blood. Rishabh, on the other hand, stood witnessing the whole event helplessly. He was dumbfounded and was in complete shock. What happened later was something he could not recollect even now. He withdrew completely from his friends and family. They were worried for him. Time heals so did Rishabh's wounds. A few months later, his life slowly returned to normalcy.

During the final year of his MBA, his parents were invited for a wedding at Ahmedabad. It was the wedding of his close NRI cousin, Kamlesh. The family had spent a fortune for the wedding.

Though Rishabh was not keen, he left for Ahmedabad on his parents' insistence. They thought meeting his cousins would cheer him up.

On the day of *sangeet*, Rishabh was lending some help to a cousin of his who was busy decorating the terrace with flowers. It was from there he first saw Payal Jain.

She got down from the car and adjusted her green colour Chaniya Choli and pulled back her long hair. She was greeted by his aunt. On an impulse, Sid left the basket of flowers behind and rushed downstairs. He saw her having an intimate conversation with the groom.

She was of medium height and wore at least three inches of heels to look taller. As he came nearer, he heard them discussing the wedding details. Seeing Rishabh, Kamlesh signalled him to come over. He introduced Rishabh to Payal. She said a quick hello and continued talking with Kamlesh. Over the conversation, he found out that she was Kamlesh's wedding planner.

As a child, Payal loved birthday parties. As she grew up, she took keen interest in designing and managing the playsets. She was the so-called event manager of her college fest activities. When asked about her career plans, she was unsure. Until one day, she met Sonali. She was a professional wedding planner. After a small talk, Sonali agreed to hire her as a trainee. Payal enjoyed her work, and she knew this was the career she wanted to take up.

She worked hard and learnt all the aspects of this trade. In no time, she became Sonali's partner.

Rishabh and Payal bumped into each other on several occasions during Kamlesh's three-day long wedding. After a long time, Rishabh laughed at jokes. He began to enjoy her company. His family noticed this. By the time Kamlesh was married, Rishabh found himself deeply attached to Payal. They kept in touch for over a year. Rishabh got a job in a private firm. They got married the following year. Payal moved her business to Mumbai.

At the office, Rishabh was popular for his four-container lunch box. Payal was an excellent cook. She would send lunch through the efficient Mumbai dabbawala. This was one tiffin which the entire office staff looked forward to, especially Sid. His craving for home-made food came to an end with Payal sending this amazing home-cooked food every day.

Sid spent most of his time with Rishabh. He was extremely knowledgeable and willing to share. Though they belonged to different divisions, the hunger to learn bonded them.

Sid embraced the fast-paced life of Mumbai well. There was a lot of travelling too. He would fly business class and live in executive suites in five-star hotels. Yes, sure, this did pay him well as his life changed significantly over the years.

The career graph jolted down by him had worked just fine. Slowly, Sid raised into the post of vice-president and Rishabh a senior associate.

Being a vice-president was not easy, but the luxuries that came with it made it worthwhile. Sid was now the owner of a BMW and a huge apartment. It was housed in an elite society in Mumbai's well-known suburbs Bandra. It was a peaceful locality. There were two apartments in each floor. He shared his floor with the Banerjees. Mr Somdutt Banerjee held a senior post in an aviation company, and his wife was a homemaker. Other than an occasional 'hello' in the lift or while picking up the morning newspaper, Sid hardly interacted with them.

The society celebrated various festivals, and *Ganesh Chaturti* was one of Sid's favourite. Sid would go the first day and offer his prayers. On the day of *Visergan* (idol immersion), he would watch the procession go by from the balcony of his apartment. He loved the enthusiasm and energy with which the young and old people would dance before the elephant God. Of course, the thunderous music could turn even a non-dancer into a dancer and put any well-known DJ to shame. There were many other events happening which Sid was hardly aware of.

Sid was engaged to a slim, tall, and beautiful girl called Kamya Khurana, who also happened to work in his office.

Kamya was a typical Sobo girl who lived with her parents in Mumbai. She was their only child. Though she was extremely popular in school and college for both her looks and intelligence, she never let any kind of distraction come her way.

Unlike Sid, she was born and brought up in the posh locality of who is who in Mumbai. She had everything, young men claiming to be in love with her, parents who absolutely adored her, and a great lifestyle.

Her father, a retired IAS officer, wanted her to clear the civil services exams and take up a government job, but she was keener on getting into the corporate world. She took up the civil exams once on his bequest and gave up later. All the young women achievers were her idols, and she dreamt of being like one of them someday.

She herself was a B-school graduate from a reputed institute in Mumbai. Her extremely ambitious and choosy nature made her turn down quite some offers. Finally, she settled for Ascii (97–122) Solutions, the reason she still wonders.

All of twenty-three, she had walked in late for the interview, but thankfully, Sid, her interviewer, had turned up late too.

It was July, the time of year when rains lashed the city. The roads were flooded. Her car had broken down the previous day and was still in the garage. She hailed for a taxi. Most of them refused to take her as the subway was flooded. Finally, she got into one of them who agreed to drop her provided she paid a little more. She agreed. It took her almost two hours to reach the office.

Wearing a formal black skirt and a grey shirt, she walked towards the reception and enquired with the receptionist. She was polite and asked her to be seated. Kamya was nervous as she waited to be called. She swept the straightened hair from her face.

A few minutes later, she was ushered into Sid's cabin. Sid liked the confidence with which she walked in. She had a commanding voice too.

Kamya was a woman of finance with razor-sharp ability to convince. When she spoke on a particular topic, she would always plan at least three steps ahead, which was a huge advantage in this industry. She was extremely knowledgeable and a very good listener, which took Sid by surprise for a young girl like her. He had interviewed many young banking aspirants but was yet to come across someone like Kamya.

The package that she put forth was a little high for an associate. But Sid knew it would be extremely foolish of him to let her go. After discussing with the management, they decided to employ her. Soon, the appointment letter followed. She joined the following day and reported to Sid.

For Kamya, it was love at first sight. As Sid spoke about the company and the nature of job she would be handling, she heard him with complete attention, and the love seemed to grow every minute. Sid loved his job, and it reflected when he spoke. It was this quality of his that had Kamya completely smitten by him.

She would seek Sid's guidance, which Sid was more than happy to give. Slowly, they got to know each other. She accompanied Sid abroad for almost all the meetings. They performed well as a team with a high success rate and cracked almost all the deals.

The only thing Sid disliked about her was the random moods on which she herself had no control over. There were times when she would argue endlessly to prove a point when maybe every other person disapproved of. But she would continue and do things that she would regret later.

But yes, none of us are perfect!

Over a period of time, somewhere between the meetings, guidance, and work, Sid fell in love with Kamya. Soon, they began dating. A few months later, over a cup of coffee, both shared their feelings for each other and were glad it was mutual.

Being in a relationship felt normal as they spent most of the time together. They wanted to give it sometime and see where it headed towards before they committed. Light and non-committed relationships were common in these days. Both were not in a hurry as they wanted to concentrate on their respective careers. Sid had intended to marry Kamya sometime until one day the company's board meeting changed their lives completely.

CHAPTER TWO

A pleasant morning welcomed Sid. Sun shone brightly. Sid had been awake the whole night, thinking about the board meeting, which was to be held a few hours from now. He had his air conditioner fixed, but sleep ceased to exist. He had tossed and turned the whole night. He kept assuring himself that everything was going to work all right.

This board meeting had been in his mind for about three months as the current Managing Director Mr Jignesh Mehta had planned to retire voluntarily and pursue something he was very passionate about, 'organic farming'.

He was in his mid-fifties and a driving force of the company. He was instrumental in bringing the company to the level it was today. It was difficult to imagine he would be gone soon. Sid greatly respected him. He had already gone through two major heart surgeries. The one that happened recently made him sit back and think. His doctors had asked him to take it easy, or a complete burnout was inevitable, they said. After the second surgery, he was a little shaken. His body felt like set organs placed at the right places held together by medical science.

He began making plans to live whatsoever was left of him peacefully. He bought a small piece of land near Kutch, Gujarat, his hometown, and did the necessary ground work so that he could begin farming soon. His family welcomed his decision, especially his only child Paresh Mehta.

He was an MBA based in Ahmedabad but living in and out of his suitcase. At the age of twenty-three, he had tied up with various budget, luxury, and ultra-luxury hotels across the country and rented rooms online. Mr Mehta was extremely proud of him. With his son doing well, he found no reason to stress himself further and decided to take up something he had wished throughout his life. His wife readily agreed. She wanted to move away from a place where everybody seemed to be racing against time.

His decision was accepted by the board and the hunt for the new managing director began. Of course, Sid had always been his choice, but apparently, he was not the only one to decide. He had to discuss with the board before they reached a conclusion. The board meeting to be held shortly was all about this.

Sid's record was impressive. His colleagues knew for sure that he would be the obvious choice for the post soon-to-be vacant.

Though he looked confident, his thoughts were somehow unsure. His concern was about a young man called Yash Bajaj, who was currently the vice-president of financing group division. He was known to be close to the board of directors.

Yash Bajaj, a thirty-seven-year-old, was an arrogant, mean, and tenacious sort of a person. He came from a well-to-do family and did not let go an opportunity to state this. He was a man with plenty of impudence. He would boast about his connections with influential families and his contacts with the people at high and mighty positions in the government. This irritated everyone in the office, especially Sid. He was a spoilt brat and a womaniser who would do anything to get a girl whom he had set his eyes on. He would spend lavishly and bore her with his accomplishments till the time she would call it quits. His girlfriends would change more or less every fortnight. He had always wanted to date Kamya but knew that she was engaged to Sid and therefore maintained distance. He was a smooth-talker and took life lightly worked where it was noticed. He loved to be in the helm of new ventures, and when he spoke, he almost sounded like a rising politician.

What bothered Sid the most was not Yash's fancy background but an incident that had taken place recently.

Sid was working for a client, an IT company, who were keen on acquiring another small company that excelled in web services. It was a product extension merger with creation of synergy being the main aim. The deal was very important to Sid as it would increase the company's profitability drastically. Sid and Kamya had worked very hard on this acquisition. The target company had excellent prospects. Hence, there were several bidders.

Sid was known for exceptional negotiation skills. He was looking forward to close the deal soon. The process typically had to begin with the acquiring company discreetly buying up shares of the target company. It looked fine as the price was steady. They had worked on the tender offer and had set up a meeting with CEO and top managers of the company to decide on the acquisition and buying of shares the following week.

On the appointed day, Sid and Kamya put forth the presentation on how this acquisition could improve the company's standing in the investment community, and like every acquisition, it went on fine till they took off for a short break. During the break, Sid found out that the target company's share price skyrocketed. He had been studying the target company's standing in the market for quite some time now. He had found no such variation.

How did this happen overnight? thought Sid.

The chances of acquisition were completely hampered. It was a face-losing situation for Sid, and the deal fell through.

In the following few days, he found out that Yash with his so-called connections fielded a few investors into buying the target company's shares. There was no concrete proof though.

The following evening, as the trio Sid, Kamya, and Rishabh were seated in a coffee shop, taking a much-needed break from the office work, Sid brought up the topic.

'Why would he do that?' Kamya asked, opening her eyes widely.

'You have to ask him,' Sid said, thinking.

'He is not the kind to interfere at least when it concerns the company's profit margin. I am perfectly certain he would not do such a thing,' said Rishabh.

'I agree,' Kamya said.

'I don't care what you both think, but I know for the fact that he did it,' Sid said.

'How could you be so sure?' Rishabh asked.

'There can be just one answer to this,' Sid said finally.

'What?' asked Rishabh.

'The soon-to-be vacant managing director's post,' said Sid.

Rishabh nodded.

'Yes, of course, he has been eyeing this for some time,' Rishabh said.

'Excatly, how could this have escaped my mind?' Kamya said.

It was unbelievable what people could do for power.

'That smug,' Sid said aloud, shaking off his thoughts.

He freshened up and wore his Armani, which he considered lucky as Kamya had picked it up for him. Today was the day when he would get to meet all the company's top brass, and he wanted to look presentable.

Once dressed, Sid headed towards his office in Bandra Kurla Complex. He absolutely adored his BMW. Its comfortable leather seats gave it a cool look. He switched on the ignition, and in seconds, the music system was turned on. Taylor Swift's voice 'Shake It Off' came to life. She was his current favourite. This kept changing like the top twenty charts of music channel. He pressed the accelerator and headed towards his office.

Kamya had arrived a little early. She was dressed in a beige skirt and a turquoise blue top. Her hair was pulled back and gathered into a pony tail. Sid walked towards her. She greeted him with a quick peck on his cheek.

'I can't wait to hear the good news,' Kamaya gushed as she wished him good luck.

Sid smiled at her happily.

She had already been planning for a promotion party and was busy preparing the guest list. Rishabh wished him too. Both made their way towards the conference room in silence.

Conference room was a huge one designed by a renowned architect with generous use of teak and marble. Sid took his seat. Rishabh sat next to him. The others sat down too. Minutes later, the chairman arrived. He was ushered to a seat in the centre. He spoke elaborately about problems that needed immediate attention. They went on to discuss various matters of importance. Sid was unable to concentrate. He saw Yash sitting across the table. He was listening with apt attention as though he would be served with a questionnaire at the end and he had planned to top it.

This made Sid smile.

The next fifteen minutes just refused to pass. Finally, they reached the most important topic in the agenda: the company's future managing director.

Sid found himself breathing heavily. Rishabh looked at Sid and nodded. The chairman stood up to make the impending announcement. The room was quiet. Everyone turned their attention towards the speaker. He began with company's various achievements and recognised Sid's contribution towards the company's business.

Sid liked this and was eager to hear the next part.

He continued speaking about the other endeavours. Time seemed to be going real slow. Soon, the name Yash Bajaj was announced as the future managing director with the consent from the board.

Sid felt hurled, beaten, and choked all at the same time.

He could not hear more as the person's words were drowned with a huge applause. Sid sensed a sickening feeling in his stomach. He found it hard to breathe. Somehow his hand reached for the mineral water bottle. After a little drink, things started settling down. His carefully planned thank-you speech had just gone down the drain. Rishabh, though taken aback, tried to look normal.

As the news of Yash being the new managing director sunk in, the sickening feeling seemed to have reappeared. Congratulatory handshakes were in order. Yash, the newly elected managing director, smiled at everyone and Sid in particular smugly.

'Congrats, dude,' Sid stammered as he shook hands with Yash, who gave him a sympathetic smile which was more of sarcasm. He had just received a much-needed ego massage. Though Sid was in too much pain, it was hard not to notice this. He strode out of the room, cursing the corporate world in general and Yash in particular.

Once out of the conference room, Sid began to breathe a little easily. He opened the window of his cabin to let in some fresh air. He looked out. The sinking feeling returned. It was around four in the evening. The air was cool. He let out a deep breath. He had never expected a day so promising to end like this.

Why was he rejected? he wondered.

Kamya walked in all worked up. She had just got the news of Yash's elevation to the post of managing director.

'This is all so disappointing, Sid. I still can't get it,' she said.

'I get it. It is that goddamn acquisition which did not happen. Now I am sure of Yash's involvement.'

'I don't think so, Sid.'

'What?'

'It is not that, Sid. You still don't get it, do you?'

'What?'

'You know, Yash, he was always polite to the board panel. He knew their opinion mattered.'

'What are you getting at?'

'I mean . . . you are straightforward. You never accept a view that is contrary to yours.'

'You mean I am not entitled to put forth an honest opinion?' Sid asked.

'Yes, of course, you are. But sometimes you need to be a little diplomatic.'

'Oh, I get. All these years while I got promoted, my honesty was the sexiest thing about me. Suddenly, the word honesty is spelt as being idiotic?'

'Why are you arguing, Sid? Can't you see how your temper has brought you down?' asked Kamya harshly.

'Oh, now I have temper too. I don't believe this. All those applauses I had received from you over the years for my disagreements with the board seem to have disappeared just because I was not promoted?' Sid asked.

'Just drop it, Sid. Talk to me when you want to have a rational conversation,' she said as she prepared to leave.

'Don't just walk away from me,' Sid said outraged.

'Look, I am not here to participate in this childish feud of yours,' Kamya said as she moved towards the door.

Sid's face turned pale. He looked like he had received a punch on his face. He had expected her empathy. They continued to argue, which slowly turned into an ugly brawl.

'They say you learn from failure, but this surely sucks, man,' Sid scowled, loosening his tie.

Seeing Sid's upset, Kamya left the room without another word.

For the first time, Sid felt that putting in hours was not enough. You'd got to spend your time on the right things and work smart.

Either way you learn, he thought.

Over the next few days, Yash, who considered Sid to be his opponent, did not let go of a single opportunity to undermine him. This did not go unnoticed by the employees in the organisation. Soon, there was group in favour of Yash and another backing Sid.

Once an employee who was known to have had this Midas touch and who could transform any disastrous project into something marvellous was today completely sidetracked from almost all the projects. He was made to look and feel useless. Working condition at the office began to deteriorate to an extent that it became extremely difficult for Sid to continue.

One of the days, Yash called in for an urgent meeting.

There were more meetings than work these days, thought Sid.

Very soon, the top executives gathered in the conference room. Yash loved it when people assembled on his command. Soon, they were all seated. Yash began to speak about how past few months had been difficult for the company. He made a special mention of Sid's undone deal with the IT company. Sid turned red.

I know you screwed it up, loser, thought Sid.

He looked at Kamya. Somehow she seemed to be keen on listening to Yash's words of wisdom.

'We need to do some changes here,' Yash said.

'So we have decided go in for a little shuffle,' he continued.

He loved to speak the same words arranged differently.

He went on with his so-called little changes and then came to the change that Sid had not dreamt off.

'We decided to shift Sid to the asset management division,' he said, looking at Sid.

Sid almost fell off his chair. How did he know his dislike towards this division? *This guy must hate me a little too much to do this,* he thought.

'Sudesh, who is the head there, is more than happy to have Sid join him,' Yash said sarcastically.

Sudesh nodded and began noting down something on his writing pad.

Never had an imaginary punch hurt Sid so much. He stared at Yash, who looked at him, smiling. He wished he could give this pig a slow painful death.

This was the last straw. He was the last one to leave the conference room. He headed straight to Yash's cabin. Yash, as usual, appeared calm with a smile that made him look like a con.

'So, Sid, happy with the new role,' he said mockingly.

How generous of you, thought Sid.

'It looks like you are happier,' said Sid.

'Oh, come on, Sid. You know how you messed up the previous acquisition. Company was entailed with additional costs to the firm for rectifying the error. This change will do you good. You have been stuck with the current division since you joined. So we decided it was time for you to take up something new,' he said as though he was genuinely concerned with his well-being.

He put it so well that it sounded like Sid was sent on a paid vacation to Mauritius. It was useless talking to him. The 'we' that he emphasised was more of an 'I'.

I could strangle him and then abscond to Mauritius, thought Sid.

'Well, Yash, in that case you leave me with no choice but to quit,' he said.

Yash had seen this coming. He shrugged and said, 'If this is what you want, I think we should let you go.'

'Well, then,' said Sid, getting up.

As Sid got up, Yash extended his hand for a handshake.

'Good luck, Sid,' said Yash, looking at him with a smile.

Sid turned and left. He felt the floor crumbling after him as he walked slowly towards his cabin. The news had already reached the entire staff. As Sid reached his cabin, the group that used to support him remained silent clearly not wanting to be a part of this.

Kamya came over a little later. As usual, her anger was evident. Though she was aware of the ongoing war between Yash and Sid, somehow she chose to blame Sid. He was completely lost in a deep thought. As he heard footsteps, he turned around. She walked towards him and placed her hand on his shoulders.

'Sid, I understand how you feel, but you are overreacting, and tending the resignation, come on, that was very immature.'

'You heard him right? Asset management? Come on.'

'You could have sorted this out.'

Sid sat, staring at his cellphone. He was hurt and had not expected this.

'How do you except me to talk to a guy who is enjoying every moment of this?' asked Sid.

Kamya was silent.

'Damn it. I was left with no option. He wants me to work under Sudesh, the guy who was trained by me. Is this not reason enough?' Sid grunted not lifting his head.

Kamya tried to persuade Sid.

Somebody had to talk some sense to him, she thought.

'Come on, Sid, it is not like you are working under Sudesh. Stop sulking.'

Sid was crushed.

Sulking, immature damn it. What is she hinting at?

It took time for him to digest the fact that even Kamya wanted him to compromise.

'Oh, well, tell me then huh . . . how it is . . . I am all ears,' spluttered Sid disbelievingly.

'Yash suggested that you work as a team, you and Sudesh.'

'Oh, a team, come on, Kamya, not you. How do you know what he meant?'

Kamya hesitated.

'I spoke to him, Sid. He told me about it. A change is always good. I think I agree with him,' she said as calmly as possible. 'You are being unreasonable.'

'Oh, wow . . . I can't believe this. Now you have small talks with that arrogant ass about me. This is news. I must say I am surprised. So what else did this enlightened soul tell you,' asked a visibly disturbed Sid.

'Sid, this is ridiculous. You are jealous of Yash . . . and you have been at sword's edge since he was promoted. Why don't you simply accept the fact that he is better than you?' said Kamya coolly.

The stream of words that were coming from her was like arrows had been aimed at him from all directions. He was hit and hurt. He could not absorb. Of course, he was envious.

'Lately, you seem to take a great deal of interest in him. Is it because you find him to be a better catch?' he questioned her and regretted almost immediately.

Kamya found this insulting. She glared at him as she moved away.

'Don't you speak to me that way, you coward. You are nothing but a selfish, immature, . . . and . . . egotistic jerk,' Kamya said in a harsh but steady voice.

Sid was unmoved. In a matter of few days, they had grown apart. He knew it was over.

In an unexpected swing of emotion, she removed her engagement ring and placed it on the table. She collected her cellphone and looked towards Sid for one last time. Sid did not look up instead he seemed to be busy checking his e-mails.

With no response from Sid, she left the place in a huff.

As Kamya left, Rishabh walked in.

He looked around clearly troubled. This had been a usual sight for some time now.

Rishabh had joined the company a few months after Sid. He had worked with both Kamya and Sid and knew both of them for a very long time. As Kamya, he too had expected Sid to be the new head. But he managed to conceal his disappointment.

Earlier, their company was something he sought out for, but with the recent developments, he found it extremely embarrassing to be there when the two were almost yelling at each other.

He waited for the awkward moment to pass. He genuinely felt sorry for Sid.

'Man, you are a complete mess.'

'I quit,' Sid said abruptly.

'I know. Everyone out there is surprised. I know about the change, but I want to hear it from you. What was the problem?' he asked.

'I could not stand the humiliation any more. That loser, he wants me to work under Sudesh. Do you believe this? And Kamya, she agrees with him.'

He was unable to follow as to what was hurting Sid the most, losing the job or Yash having snaked his girlfriend.

'I understand, Sid. Let us get out of here and hit the bar. You will feel better.'

Sid was in no mood. Having lost his job and girlfriend, he wanted to be left alone. The thought of Kamya approving Yash's decision made it even worse.

'Thanks, man. I would rather be alone than be in a company of people who by now would know about my resignation. They would either distance themselves from me or prod into it deeper. I am in no mood for this. I have faced enough humiliation for the day. I want to go somewhere quiet,' Sid replied, getting up.

Rishabh did not press further.

Sid quietly packed his stuff and put them into a cardboard box. Rishabh helped him with it. Many of his colleagues wanted to stop by and wish him. He refused to talk to them.

To pretend that nothing had happened was tough. For past eight years, this cabin had been his home. The window of his cabin overlooked a huge Gulmohar tree. It would look lovely during the spring when it would shed its leaves and the tree with almost no leaves resembled a huge red fountain. He would reach the office every morning by 8.30 a.m. sharp and would leave late after sunset. He had never once taken leave except for a week when his grandpa was admitted to the hospital having suffered a stroke. The cabin held lot of memories. Huge decisions were made here. The cabin was a witness to the late-night work, smiles of satisfaction, and celebrations of his team's success. It had many tall stories to tell.

During the monsoon, one of the days due to heavy rains, he had spent an entire night here. This was the very room where he had first met Kamya.

He stood up and took a deep breath.

'I never thought I would be leaving like this,' he said.

'I know. I don't believe this,' Rishabh replied.

After some time, having done with packing, he said looking around, 'That's it, I guess.'

'I guess so. Let me help you carry the stuff,' Rishabh said, carrying a cardboard box.

'Thanks,' Sid replied.

He slowly collected his stuff and gave one last look to his cabin.

Both of them made their way towards the parking lot, avoiding every person on their way. Rishabh put the box into the luggage space of the car.

Sid sat down on the driver's seat and thanked Rishabh again. Rishabh wished Sid and promised to keep in touch.

CHAPTER THREE

As Rishabh left, Sid felt alone. He drove out of the building with hurt and self-pity. Seated in his BMW, Sid wanted to move far away from the overcrowded city. Normally, his thoughts would have been on how he could maximise profitability of his company. But today, it was different. He could think just about anything he wanted to and go anywhere he wished to. He stopped as the signal turned red and looked out of the window.

For the first time, he noticed people around. As usual, traffic was heavy. There was a boy selling pirated books, another boy selling flowers, and another trying to sell a sun-shield to a man in an SUV. He also seemed to be giving a demo to the person who was not so convinced. Sid smiled. He wondered there were so many means of livelihood.

Sid drove aimlessly, zipping between the cars. As he moved further, he glanced at the rear-view mirror and saw the city move away from him. He reached the Mumbai–Pune expressway. He felt a little better. After driving for a while, he took a diversion from the expressway. It was a small connecting road, which was way too narrow for heavy vehicles. The road ahead was a mud road. After an hour's drive, he was exhausted.

As he drove, his thoughts returned to the day's turn of events. He deliberately tried to put them away. But they came back with more force.

Yes, it was difficult and painful. He half-closed his eyes. He could see Yash's face beaming and Kamya trying to be a little more than nice to Yash. When a relationship breaks, you ponder all situations.

The party that she had planned to host for Sid would now be held in Yash's honour, of course with a little alteration in the guest list. Rishabh and Payal might be there too. After all, they worked together. Maybe his place was already taken.

He was unable to manage the wheel any more. Soon, he lost control, and his beloved BMW hit a tree with a loud bang. His head began to spin as the vehicle smashed the tree trunk. The air bags opened up. With few scratches here and there, Sid escaped unhurt. It took some time for things to settle down.

Sid lifted his head slowly. As he tried to move forward, there was a sharp pain in his back. He shrieked in agony, his back hurt like hell. He rested for a while and breathed deeply. Slowly, he unfastened his seat belt and stumbled out of the car to inspect the level of damage. His car seemed to be in a very bad condition. He checked his Swiss watch; it was 7.30 p.m. He looked around for help. The place was secluded. All he could see was upright trees staring back at him. He slammed the door with disgust.

The eeriness of the place was increased by the dirt road ahead, which looked completely abandoned. Not knowing what to do, he reached out for his smartphone. He punched the car service number. After a few rings, he got connected.

Citing his location, the person at the desk informed him that it would take at least three to four hours to reach him. Hearing this, an already agitated Sid began a heated argument.

'What the hell is this? God, I don't believe this. Three to four hours, are you crazy? You want me to simply wait here for four hours. Oh, wonderful! I mean what age are we in Stone Age?' Sid burst out.

Despite his rudeness, the person at the other end heard him out tolerantly.

We can't possibly send a parachute and fly this person home, he thought as he waited for Sid to cool down.

Little later, calming down considerably, 'Could you not do something about this . . . uh-huh . . . like get me out of here sooner? I mean this place looks totally spooky,' Sid continued looking around.

'Sir, I am sorry you have to go through this, but you are four hours away from the city, and it would take us a few hours to reach,' he answered patiently.

Sid disconnected the phone, swearing, 'What the hell?' and hit a stone in frustration. The stone landed near a milestone.

'This is not the way to speak to a person who is trying to help you,' said a voice from somewhere behind.

Sid turned around to see the source of the voice.

A man in starched white kurta and pyjama emerged from nowhere. His voice was silvery. He had some kind of aura about himself. He was of wheatish complexion. His eyes were bright and kind. He had a thick matt of jet-black hair. He was a little over six feet and seemed to tower over Sid.

He looked around and slowly sat down comfortably on a milestone and flashed a confident smile.

Sid looked at this strange man blankly.

'Who the hell are you? How come you are in this place? As far as I can see, there seems to be no sign of habitation whatsoever. It looks like you appeared out of thin air. Are you a passer-by?' Sid blurted out.

The man seated on the milestone heard Sid out.

'My my, you have so many questions. Why are you so impatient? Nobody likes a person with bad temper.'

Sid was not pleased so he continued staring at him. The man watched and waited.

'Yes, of course, I appeared just the way you described,' said the man.

Sid continued to stare at him. There was a sharp pain in his back. He stroked his back.

'What do you mean?' Sid said as he tried to smoothen the pain in his back, which seemed to have suddenly reappeared.

'Like I said I appear when it is required.'

'Ohm sure,' said Sid sarcastically.

'Rough day, huh?'

Sid let a short laugh. Maybe he was seeing things.

You have no idea, Sid thought.

'Yes, quite a day. Seriously, don't tell me you are God and you have come to save me.'

'Yes, I am his *Dhoot* just like messenger you use these days.'

'Look, I had a long day. You don't know what I have been through. So please either you help me or you just leave,' Sid replied exhausted.

'Of course, I know what you have been through. You have lost your job, so-called girlfriend, and now the accident, quite a day, son,' the man said knowingly.

Sid was shocked. *How did he know this?* he thought.

'Are you some kind of a spy sent by Yash?' Sid said cautiously.

The man grinned.

'Oh, come on, the guy must be partying somewhere.'

'I know,' Sid said sadly.

'I come when it is needed. Look, I have a job to do, which is to see that you are fine till the time the car service people arrive and pick you up. I understand it will take four hours for them to reach. So meanwhile, let us be cordial to each other,' the man said.

Sid thought maybe he was seeing things and due to the recent happenings could not think sane. Anyway, he was all alone here, and there was not a single flicker of light except for the moonlight, and the deathly stillness sacred him.

I might as well have some company, he thought.

'Some other day, maybe I would have reacted differently, but not today. Pleasure meeting you, hum . . .

What do I call you? Say . . . let me call you *Dhootji*. How do you like that?' Sid said smiling.

'*Dhootji*! Yes, sounds good. People call me by different names. Ultimately, I am all the same,' *Dhootji* replied.

Sid smiled. *This is all so lame*, he thought, shaking his head.

'To begin with, *Dhootji*, you know everything about me, so introductions are a sheer waste of time. So let me begin by asking you, how did you know I was in trouble? I never asked God for help,' Sid asked.

'Son, whether you call me or not, it does not matter. My job, just like the one you lost, is to look after you. I am just like a messenger, you know the messengers you use these days to communicate,' *Dhootji* replied.

'*Dhootji*, you?' Sid asked surprised.

'Son, there is nothing in this world I don't know of. We too need to keep ourselves up to date, isn't it?' *Dhootji* said, smiling.

Sid nodded.

Meanwhile, his phone began to ring. He looked at *Dhootji* and said, 'I need to take this.'

'Yes, of course, it is your mother,' *Dhootji* said.

Sid shook his head. This time not too surprised.

After a moment, he answered the call. On the other end, his worried mom spoke breathlessly, 'Siddu, *Beta*, how are you? I am so worried. Please take care of yourself. I had told you earlier this hep girl you are roaming around with is not the one for you. But you never listen. See, what has happened to you. How could she be so insensitive? *Beta*, take the first flight to Chandigarh.

Come and stay with us for a few days and heal. Being with us will make it easier to get over the pain. We will all try and sort out the matter. Just remember, son, we are there for you no matter what.'

Sid let out a sigh.

Before Sid could answer, the cellphone battery was down, and the conversation ended abruptly. Sid cursed.

'What the heck?' Sid said, keeping the phone back in his pocket.

'How the hell did she know about the break-up?'

Dhootji grinned slightly.

'Ten minutes after you both decided to end the relationship, your ex has changed her Facebook status to single and sent around a post saying, "Feeling low after break-up ☹☹☹☹".'

Sid did not bother to ask how this person knew of this.

'This is crazy. I can't believe this. I have still not come to terms regarding this, and that bloody b***h has the cheek to go around circulating this news via social network.'

'Son, this is not the way you speak of women though I know she has hurt you,' *Dhootji* said sternly.

Sid nodded.

'You will not believe there are people who go around pressing *like* for whatsoever post. She already has 272 likes and 169 comments as to how? when? why? take care, and so on . . . . . . Comments maybe, but I fail to understand how someone can *like* a post that displays so much sadness.'

'"Like" is an *acknowledgement* of some sorts not the literal meaning, *Dhootji,* and with the latest version, they have more emoticons,' Sid corrected.

'Anyway, I am sure the next thing on her status would be "Found someone special . . .☺☺☺☺ Over the moon, blah . . . blah". So let go of her, Son.'

Sid hung his head in shame.

'Is there no emotions at all?' he asked faintly.

'Oh, there are many in the form of emoticons. One for every word,' *Dhootji* replied, almost smiling.

'This is not funny, *Dhootji.* I mean I dated her for past two and half years, and she did not spend a few minutes just to think about what went wrong or is it possible to work it out somehow. I thought we had something,' Sid said sadly.

'Patience, Son, patience, your generation lacks this. They want results instantly. Love, marriage, break-up are mere words spoken or put on the Internet. When you speak of the word love, it is a loaded word, expressing commitment. Most of them live a complete virtual social life, connecting to unknown people and neglecting the ones physically present with them,' *Dhootji* said matter-of-factly.

Sid agreed. He removed the phone from his pocket.

'God, I don't know how far the car service person is. Now this damn thing is not working,' said Sid.

Dhootji asked Sid to give his phone. Sid handed over the instrument unwillingly.

'There is no charge,' Sid said.

Dhootji smiled at him. He held it in his hand for a few seconds, and the instrument came to life.

Sid was shocked.

'Oh, Wow! That was cool,' Sid said.

There was a brief moment of silence; unsure if he should continue, Sid said, 'Do you really mean that . . . ', he paused for a while, 'I mean . . . you know what . . .' Sid fumbled as he spoke.

Dhootji nodded.

'Yes, sadly, I have to prove my existence time and again. If you had your way, you would develop an app called God and open it only when you are in misery,' said *Dhootji*.

Sid smiled and nodded his head knowingly. He tried calling the service person but could not get through.

Not having anything to do, *Dhootji* looked at his phone contact list. Sid had around 500 contacts saved.

'How many do you know personally or have you met? Or let me put it this way: "Is there anyone who would come here to help you out?"' *Dhootji* asked.

Sid gave him a bored look.

'I don't know, *Dhootji*. Most of them are just contacts for business and some mere acquaintances. Maybe I have met them at parties and must have had a small chat not that I remember them in person. But today, I think I would call only my mom as I know she would come looking for me anywhere in this world.'

'The irony is that this is one phone call you have never answered without swearing,' *Dhootji* said.

Sid agreed.

Sid's phone started ringing, and this time it was the car service person asking for his exact location. Sid pointed out where he was to the person and hung up.

'Since the person will be there shortly, it is time to say good-bye, Sid,' said *Dhootji.*

Sid felt some kind of emptiness within him, like a lost child from Mulk Raj Anandji's story. Somehow he did not want him to go. Pretending to be relieved, he moved towards *Dhootji.*

'Speaking to you, *Dhootji,* I . . . I don't know. I mean I felt nice. It was like I have known you forever though I have met you for the first time. I wish I could spend some more time with you,' Sid said with complete honesty.

Dhootji smiled at him. Sid noticed he looked striking when he smiled,

'Don't get emotional, Son. I am always with you. It is just that you don't have time for me. You call me sincerely, and I will be there for you,' *Dhootji* replied.

'If you were with me all the time, then how come I did not see you?' Sid asked.

'You were too self-involved to see me. Today, for the first time in your life, you were miserable. People think of me only when they are distressed. It's fine, but you know it feels nice if people remember me when they are happy as well.'

Dhootji winked at him and vanished into the night.

Meanwhile, the car service team arrived. The person in charge inspected the amount of damage. It was in a bad shape. They were left with no option but to tow the car. Soon, they drove Sid back home. On his way back,

Sid kept thinking of this strange encounter; little did he know that this was going to change his life forever. He was exhausted and simply wanted to reach home as quickly as possible. He slowly drifted off to sleep. As the city lights approached, he was awoken by the service person.

He was dropped home. His apartment building was dark and quiet. He slowly entered the lift. He reached his floor and walked towards his apartment. He opened the door and, as usual, checked the telephone for messages. Once a corporate honcho, with at least fifty urgent messages that required immediate attention, he had none today. He was dejected but tried to dismiss the thoughts. He took a warm bath, which gave him a little relief. The soreness seemed to have slightly increased. Shrugging, Sid went to bed after consuming a sleeping pill.

CHAPTER FOUR

Sid's home was a four-bedroom apartment in Bandra, one of the well-known suburbs of Mumbai. Earlier, it looked like a bachelor's pad. Sid liked his home to be simple and neat. Sid's work took him to different countries, and he would always bring back an artefact from the place he had travelled to as a souvenir. He had a particular corner of his home meant for this art collection of his.

But it turned out that Kamya had a complete different taste, and she wanted a professional to do their home.

'When people ask us who did our home, what are you going to say, Sid? Come on, let us hire a reputed home decor,' said Kamya, her eyes lightening up.

Sid was way too occupied with other things and showed no interest.

Kamya had called a friend of hers and fixed an appointment with some well-known decorator. She had a reputation of turning any wreck into a marvel.

Sid would constantly postpone this appointment. After their regular clash, Sid gave his consent. An elated Kamya called the home decor immediately, and within a few months, Sid's home was turned into what he laughingly called a 'museum'. For first few months, living in the so-called museum felt strange, but later, he got used to it.

Early next morning, the alarm went off. He snoozed it and went back to sleep. After around five snoozes, he reluctantly got out of the bed.

The doorbell rang. It was his maid Nitya.

'*Saab*, you have taken a holiday or . . . ? Are you unwell?' Nitya asked, looking at his appearance.

Taking an off from the office was something which Sid had never done in the past seven years. He had been working even during the weekends until recently ever since Kamya came into his life. They would spend a quiet weekend at a nearby getaway either alone or sometimes with Rishabh and Payal.

Sid told Nitya he had quit the job and that he was going to be at home for some time now.

'Oh, don't worry, *Saab*, you will get a better one soon,' Nitya replied confidently as though she was a HR consultant.

After handing over coffee to Sid, she went around doing her household chores amidst laughing and talking over the cellphone.

Sid wondered whom she was conversing with.

Nitya was an independent woman who had been working for Sid since he had shifted to this apartment. As the time passed by, she knew Sid's choice of food and cooked accordingly. She was punctual and hardly gossiped. She was a single mother and had two sons to care for. She singlehandedly took care of their education and provided them with things she could afford.

When her elder son Anmol wanted a laptop, Sid had given his old one, which was not of much use to him. She was so grateful that she brought her son to thank Sid personally. And she went on to say that 'One day you have to become like Saab' for which the son nodded. Sid was touched and gave him a few of his designer clothes, which he took gratefully. She took loan from Sid every now and then. But she was careful enough not to take without completing the previous one.

She had enrolled her son in a computer institute where he fared well and got a decent job. The day he received his first salary, he gifted Sid with a polyester shirt, which Nitya handed over with huge pride. Though Sid never wore it, he kept it with him. For Sid, Nitya was an example of women empowerment.

Sid sat down sipping his coffee. While he was reading the day's edition of *Financial Times*, Nitya appeared at his doorway.

'*Saab,* I have cooked both lunch and dinner. I am leaving now,' Nitya said.

Sid smiled and nodded.

He flipped through the newspaper. After reading the headlines, he put it away. He had light breakfast. Taking a quick shower and not knowing what to do next, Sid took a stroll in the apartment garden. Unsure of his future, he walked out of his building. He hailed the first available taxi and headed towards Marine drive. He lumbered along the so-called Queen's Necklace for some time.

Sea was a place he retracted to when he was unable to comprehend. He loved to watch the intensity at which the waves arrived only to hit the shore and calm down.

He looked around for an eatery. There was a cafe in the corner. He walked into the cafe. It was almost 12 noon, and the restaurant began filling. He ordered coffee and then another and finally left the place. He walked for some time, trying to think clearly. By late afternoon, he was tired and made his way back home.

At home, Sid checked his phone for messages. There are none, except for a few call centre guys offering him loan or some kind of credit card. He took a quick shower and lay on his bed lost in deep thoughts.

This went on for nearly a fortnight. With no job offers as yet, Sid felt wound up. The bruises from the wreck had almost gone, but spasms were still there.

One fine morning, his sprits lifted as he received a call from Rishabh asking him to meet up for lunch. This was something Sid wanted badly, someone to talk to. He reached the place well in advance and waited eagerly for Rishabh.

Rishabh arrived a little later. He apologised. After a quick exchange of greetings, they ordered for coffee. Sid told him about the accident. Rishabh was genuinely concerned. He enquired Sid of his health.

'I am grateful of having survived in one piece,' he said, smiling.

He informed Sid of the latest happenings at the office. Though Sid was not concerned any more, he still had a soft corner for Kamya.

'It was over a long time ago, Sid. She is currently seeing Yash,' Rishabh said, reading his thoughts.

'Damn it, I was engaged to her, Rishabh. Of all the people . . . Yash, that stupid runt, the man whom she hated as much as I did. I can't believe this,' said Sid, raging with anger.

'Forget it, Sid. I think you should get a job and move on,' said Rishabh.

It seemed so easy for Rishabh to say. His back was sore as was his heart. *How could someone 'move on' so quickly? Maybe life is too short to waste time thinking over a bad relationship.*

Meanwhile, a waiter brought two cups of coffee.

An odd look passed over Sid's face as Rishabh continued.

'There is this Mr Choudhary who would love to have you work for his company.'

Mr Choudhary was one of their competitors. He had met him a couple of times in some seminars. He was a big man, owning many other successful business ventures. Somehow Sid did not want to work for companies who were once his competitors. He more or less knew most of them, and moving around in the same old circles made him uneasy. This, of course, narrowed down his chances considerably.

'No, I don't think that is a good idea,' Sid said.

'Why not?'

'I don't know.'

'Come on, Sid. You need to pull yourself together and make up your mind. Do not let this incident consume you.'

Sid nodded thoughtfully.

'How about setting up a consulting firm?'

'That is a good idea. But what about the funds?'

'Arranging funds should not be a problem. We can take help from the bank. I mean you have enough experience and contacts,' Rishabh said hopefully.

Sid had considered this earlier. Something seemed to be holding him back. He never regretted that he quit the job. For some time now, it had lost its charm. The thought of again getting back to the daily grind was unsettling. He wanted to do something different, and he was unable to figure out what was it.

Sid suddenly felt ill. The throbbing pain in his back reappeared. His head felt heavy and dizzy. He had visuals of various people in his life, a sarcastic Yash, unapologetic Kamya, and phony staff of Ascii (97–122) solutions seemed to appear one after the other like a PowerPoint presentation in full speed. They stared at him mocking. The news of Kamya seeing Yash seemed to have an adverse effect on him. He was completely torn up inside. The pain continued, and at some point of time, he was unable to bear any more. He raised his hand trying to call out for help but fell of the chair and collapsed on to the floor.

Rishabh put down his cup and looked at him terrified. He looked around for help. Just then a waiter aided Rishabh, and together, they lifted Sid and put him down in a comfortable position.

Soon, an alarmed Rishabh called for an ambulance and took Sid to a nearby hospital. He was taken inside the room instantly. A young and beautiful doctor called Naina was in charge. After seeing Sid, she walked out and spoke to Rishabh.

'He is suffering from severe inflammation. Do not worry he will be all right soon,' she said.

Rishabh explained Naina about Sid's recent mishap.

Sid was kept under observation for twenty-four hours. He regained his conscious within a few hours. The pain was replaced by a slight discomfort. He was under severe medications. Rishabh was by his side and checked on him every now and then. Sid forbade Rishabh from informing his parents as they would worry unnecessarily.

The following day, on seeing a considerable improvement, Sid was discharged. He wanted to thank the doctor who had treated him but was told that it was her day off. Sid left a message thanking her and decided to meet her when he would come for a follow-up after ten days.

CHAPTER FIVE

Back from the hospital, Sid craved for company. Dealing with one setback after another in the last few days, Sid felt completely drained. His mind was occupied by Kamya's betrayal most of the time. He tried to convince himself that it was his fault too. But it was a lie he could not pull off well. He had been a good boyfriend and careful not to offend Kamya in any way. But he had failed though.

He never forgot her birthday. He sent her flowers with a lovely note on certain significant milestones in her career. Everything seemed to be going well for them until the board meeting. He had never thought that a day would come when she would leave him for someone like Yash, whom on several occasions had said that she detested him thoroughly.

The medications made him drowsy. He tried to shake off Kamya from his thoughts. He slowly walked towards the kitchen and prepared coffee. Sipping his coffee by the balcony, Sid recollected the day he met *Dhootji* and the wonderful time he had with him.

Was it real or was my mind playing games? Sid thought. Meanwhile, a pigeon appeared from nowhere passed by Sid very closely. Sid almost dropped the coffee mug.

'Oh God,' he said, keeping the coffee mug on the side table.

'You took a very long time to remember me,' said a familiar voice.

Yes, it is Dhootji, he thought, turning around.

Sid was shocked and happy at the same time.

Dhootji smiled at him.

'You have a lovely house, nice interiors too,' he said looking around.

Sid nodded and said that he was happy to see him.

He made himself comfortable on a cane chair.

'No luck with job, right?' he asked.

'Not yet.'

Dhootji paused and continued, 'Kamya, not surprising?'

Sid nodded.

'So what are your plans now?'

'I don't know. I see things differently now.'

'Like?'

'Let me ask you something. Don't you get tired doing the same thing, *Dhootji,* you know, meeting people like me and listening to their goddamn life story that you already know?'

'I do.'

'So what do you do about it?'

'I take a break occasionally.'

They smiled. The conversation he was having right now sounded so weird.

'You must have come up with something. There is little satisfaction in sitting idle,' said *Dhootji,* breaking the silence.

'Oh, there is nothing I can do right now. Since I graduated from B-school, I have been working my ass off for Ascii (97–122) Solutions. It meant everything to me you know "My world". I had never ever thought of a life without Ascii (97–122) Solutions.'

'Now that you do not work there any more, it is time you started thinking.'

'It is kind of tough to start something on my own. Actually, I don't want that kind of job anymore.'

'But you loved your job, right?'

'Sure, I did. You know, *Dhootji,* earlier, the sheer thought of revenue generation would give me high. But now it is the thing of past. For the first time in my life, I am confused. Maybe you would be able to help me there,' Sid said.

Dhootji was thinking deeply.

'I am always there to help, but what is it you are looking for you need to be sure. So think about it and let me know at the same time tomorrow,' said *Dhootji.*

Sid nodded. As he looked up, *Dhootji* had vanished into thin air.

Late in the night, Sid pondered, *What is that I really wanted in life?* There were numerous things he would want to do. After a through introspection, he arrived at a list of things he would ask for in the morning. He lay awake for hours, later took his pills, and retired for the night.

Chirping of the birds announced the arrival of a new day. It was unusually bright and a sunny morning. Nitya came by and completed her chores. Having finished his breakfast, Sid headed towards the balcony anxiously. At the determined time, *Dhootji* appeared. Eagerness on Sid's face was apparent.

Dhootji smiled at Sid's enthusiasm.

'You look like a child waiting for his birthday present. Or is it that you have started enjoying my company?'

'Oh, *Dhootji,* I have told you how I like unburdening myself to you. You are the only one I have,' Sid said winking.

'Little sleep last night, I guess?'

'Yep, you don't need to guess. I have made a list of all the things I want.'

Dhootji smiled at him knowingly.

'Son, I know your list, and it's quite impressive. But you know, it does not work that way. I need you to think hard and decide upon three things of utmost importance to you from the list you have made.'

'Oh.'

Sid thought for a while.

'I think I know the three things that are most important to me right now,' Sid said.

'Go ahead.'

'First, I need to get a job that I would love to do. . . . (thinks).'

'Yes, you cannot be unoccupied for long.'

'Then, maybe a partner. I mean a woman who understands me and with whom I could share my feelings.'

'Yes, of course.'

'Finally (thinks a little harder), of course, peace of mind. Yes, these are the three things I want,' Sid declared.

Hearing this, *Dhootji* nodded his head.

'Whatever luxuries one may be surrounded with, he will always find his happiness incomplete unless he has the above three.'

Sid was happy for once they seemed to have agreed upon something.

'I can make this happen,' said *Dhootji* coolly.

'You do?' asked Sid surprised.

Dhootji nodded.

'Look, Son, nothing comes free of cost. If I am giving you these three boons, then I will ask for three things from you as well,' *Dhootji* continued.

Sid looked at him curiously.

'You are the supreme, the giver. How can you ask for something? I mean, I have heard mythological stories from my grandpa that as far as I know, you have never asked anything in return. I mean, do you have some kind of a deal or are you benefiting something from this?'

'Yes, of course, Son. Benefit is not the right word. Save is more like it. Deeply introspect the stories you have heard. You will know that each one had its own consequences. This is the twenty-first century where humans are more into being open and how actually they feel. So I thought it was better this way.'

Sid nodded, and *Dhootji* smiled.

'Fair enough,' said Sid.

'Were you happy with the job you had earlier?' asked *Dhootji*.

'I used to be happy. At least I had made myself believe that. But now I think I have outgrown it.'

'Well, then let us get you a job first.'

'Sounds great. What is it?'

'Well, will you work for me?'

'What?'

'I have a job for you, and I would be glad if you would take it up.'

'I mean, I don't know what to say. Actually, it depends on what it is all about.'

'The task I am putting you into is to be the mouthpiece for 125 crores of Indians. I know it is huge, but I assure you it is going to be worth it.'

Sid hung on to every word he had to say, wondering what was this person getting him into.

'What are you talking about? I don't get it,' he asked finally.

'Well, things I am going to ask for would be something which would save the mankind from further destruction. The three boons would be given to you in exchange of three things I want from all the Indians,' *Dhootji* said.

'The give and take is to be between me and you, right?'

'Of course, it is between us,'

'So why do we have to bring the entire population into this?'

'Saving humankind is not singular. It is got to be plural.'

'I mean, how I can shoulder the responsibility of 125 crores of Indians? How can I speak for them? I mean, what makes you think I am capable of doing this?' Sid asked, studying *Dhootji* more closely.

Dhootji, who was fidgeting with a laptop on the table, could not help but laugh.

'Sid, you are capable of much more . . . rather all of them put together. The returns for the boon I am asking for is to save life, so it involves everyone. It is not going to be just about you anymore. You are here to save humanity, that is the real meaning of your existence. So I suggest you take up this mahout task though let me warn you it is going to be anything but easy,' *Dhootji* said.

He paused and opened a picture from his desktop and looked at a confused Sid.

'Are you nervous, Son?' asked *Dhootji*.

'Yes, I am,' admitted Sid.

'Look, I will not pressurise you. Think over it carefully and let me know tomorrow at the same time,' *Dhootji* said.

As he prepared to leave, he looked at the pic on his laptop for the second time and enquired about the girl in it.

'Oh, she is Naina, Naina Soni.'

'Oh,' he said, waiting for him to continue.

'She is a doctor by profession. My mother had chosen her for me,' Sid said.

Naina! thought Sid.

She was a simple and beautiful girl who enjoyed smallest of small things in life. She was born in Chandigarh and was schooled in various places like Sid as her father was in the army. She had an elder brother Amit Soni, who followed their father's footstep and joined the navy. Having completed her MBBS in Chandigarh, she was residing with her brother Amit, who was posted in Mumbai. She was pursuing her MD here. She was twenty-six, and her parents were looking forward to see her settled.

Sid's mother happened to meet Naina's parents at Chandigarh during a *Satsang,* where both the families frequented. The concern for the wedding of their respective wards brought them closer. During one such occasion, Sid's mother had seen Naina and liked her immediately. They had later exchanged pictures of their children. Though Naina was open to meeting Sid in Mumbai, Sid had flatly refused as he was seeing Kamya at that time.

'I know that . . . and . . . ?' *Dhootji* said, snapping his fingers.

'And . . . what? I was engaged to Kamya and hence refused to meet her. Come on, *Dhootji,* you know all this.'

'It is amusing to hear from you. Go on.'

Sid stared at *Dhootji.* He laughed.

'My mother was upset for a few days. She threatened to disown me, and you know all that drama.

"'I will die . . .'

"'How I could have given birth to a son like you . . . ?'

"'Is this the way I brought you up . . . ?'

"'Is it not your duty to make your parents happy . . . ?'

"'Where do you think you are living? This is India where children are supposed to listen to elders without questioning them . . .'

"'I am your mother. I know which girl suits you better . . .'

"'How I wish I had a daughter instead . . .'

"'You will never find a better girl, blah, blah,'" Sid went on uninterested.

'She is gorgeous though and looks more like a model,' *Dhootji* said looking at the pic.

'I know,' Sid said letting a sigh.

'Oh, that is sad. Anyway, make up your mind and let me know tomorrow.'

Dhootji disappeared.

It was late in the night, and Sid was unable to sleep. It was hours before dawn. There were two people talking to him endlessly in favour or not in favour of *Dhootji*'s proposal.

Something deep within him said he should take up the so-called work as he had nothing to do and maybe it would interest him and give him an opportunity to do something different. But there was another voice contradicting, trying to caution him, telling him to stay away from this as it could be dangerous, and fear pervaded his senses.

He kept thinking.

What could Dhootji ask for? Maybe some of the luxuries I enjoyed would be taken away in exchange to the boons given to me. What type of luxury? he thought.

'Maybe my car, house, or little wealth I have gathered over the years. There is nothing else he can possibly ask for,' he said to himself.

What if he asks for my life or maybe my dear ones?

The thought made him feel sick.

Dhootji seemed too benevolent to do something so unkind.

Sid knew he was stepping into the unknown. It was both exhilarating and scary at the same time. He had gone through the so-called the worst phase of his life: criticism, rejection, failure to make it to the top, and finally giving up everything. He had seen it all. This was a brilliant opportunity to embrace something new.

The fight continued, and finally the strong unconfirmed belief that this would save the mankind prevailed and Sid gave in.

CHAPTER SIX

Sid woke up late the following morning with extraordinary energy. He opened the window of his bedroom and let the breeze in. It was bright and sunny outside. The brightness of the morning seemed to have lifted up his spirits. Having decided upon taking up the task, he looked forward to meet *Dhootji*.

Dhootji appeared at the appointed time, looking calm and composed as always.

Sid smiled at him.

Though he knew of Sid's decision, he wanted to hear it from him.

'So what you decided, Son?' he asked.

While Sid spoke, *Dhootji* sat reclined on a cane chair.

'I am ready to take up this task, *Dhootji*,' Sid said, self-assured.

'Are you sure you want to do this?'

'Damn well, I do.'

'I am giving you one last chance to change your decision.'

Sid thought for a moment.

Dhootji looked up and waited for his reaction.

Sid got up from his chair and moved around nervously.

Sid was very aggressive by nature. As a child, he loved challenges. He had won many competitions for coming out with unique ideas that made the judges wonder as to how a boy so young could come up with something like this.

Later on in college, he would take up projects that were turned down by others and would work tirelessly and make them successful. This along with his charm worked for him at Ascii Solutions too.

Today, the thought of getting this so-called power to speak for all the Indians gave him a high. If it would help humankind as *Dhootji* put it, it was worth the risk. He simply wanted to take it up maybe out of sheer curiosity to know what would come next.

He always wanted to do things differently; maybe this was precisely his chance, and he was sure he did not want it to slip by.

Sid rubbed his palm and looked at *Dhootji* decisively.

'I am in, *Dhootji*. Let us begin,' Sid volunteered.

'You will not be able to back out at any stage.'

'Yes, indeed.'

'I will not be able to help since I am only a messenger and answerable to Almighty.'

Sid nodded knowingly and said he had already decided and would not change his mind now.

Dhootji cleared his throat and began.

'Now that you have agreed, let us begin this roller coaster ride. First things first, let me layout the ground rules.'

Sid nodded obediently.

'Rule one, I will grant you three boons that you have asked for, and in return you will be the voice of 125 crores of Indians and give me three things I ask for.'

Sid agreed.

'Rule two, you cannot back out under any circumstances because I cannot do anything about it and go ahead with taking what I want and giving you the three things you have asked for.'

Sid agreed.

'It will be in the span of a month with ten days gap for each beginning from today.'

Sid nodded.

Dhootji stood up and moved in circles taking time.

'You are currently out of work, right?'

'Yes.'

'I have already offered you a job.'

'Yes.'

'Think about it, Son. You are going to be the voice of 125 crores of Indians henceforth. That is, you would be speaking on behalf of them. If you handle this correctly, it would be an extraordinary opportunity.'

His voice was clear and precise. Sid nodded.

'Now that I have agreed to be a part of it, do I have a choice?' asked Sid smiling.

Dhootji smiled.

'You have given me work to do, so what is it you want in return?' Sid asked.

Dhootji was quiet.

'So what is it that you ask for?' Sid asked impatiently.

'Impatient as always, huh,' *Dhootji* said.

Sid waited.

'I want plastic to be taken away from this country,' *Dhootji* said without blinking.

Sid narrowed his eyebrows, thought for a few seconds, and said, 'Plastic?'

'Yes.'

'What do you mean?'

'I meant what I just said, Sid. I don't think it is difficult to understand.'

'And why would you want that?' he demanded.

'Cleanliness.'

'Are you out of your mind?' Sid cried.

'No.'

'Do you know everything as small as a say . . .'

Sid looked around for something to help him complete the sentence. He saw a cup of coffee.

'Packets of milk to credit cards are made of plastic. It is just not possible to replace them.'

Dhootji nodded.

'You have made it irreplaceable,' said *Dhootji*.

By now Sid was irritated; he shrugged. He had juggled between car, house, and money the previous night and was totally unprepared for something like this.

'Of all the things you want "plastic"? You know it is not possible. Why don't you ask for something else? Like maybe . . .' Sid was at loss of words.

'Nothing is impossible. Get out of the sorry state, Son. India which boosts of highly educated people requires the prime minister of the country to spread awareness regarding cleanliness. You people should be ashamed of yourselves. The way you throw garbage around and leave it there, I feel I have not bathed for days. Will you do that to yourself? Just walk out your house without bathing for a week and tell me how it feels. I am feeling the same way right now.'

He was quick to see the point. This was true.

'I agree, but this is different,' Sid said.

'How is it different? Will you not feel embarrassed if your house is full of crap and a friend comes over all of a sudden? I feel the same way when foreigners come and visit me. There was a time when I was proud. Let me tell you, Son, the aerial view of all this is really bad.'

Sid felt thoroughly ashamed. Sid had travelled abroad on various occasions. He had lot of offers to settle down aboard. But somehow he did not take it up as he loved his country immensely.

Each time he would visit a country, he would wonder how beautiful and clean it looked. On his way back, he would wonder why my country could not be like that? Was there something I could do?

After a few days, he would get busy with his work and forget about it. He would only think about this on his way back from another visit to overseas.

Sid's thoughts were interrupted by *Dhootji*.

'There are nations where people are monitored 24/7. How does it feel, Sid, to be under constant surveillance?'

'Uneasy?'

'Yes, initially uneasiness and later fear. It is like living with constant apprehension. The biggest gift this country has given to its people is freedom. It is high time you realise this. You have misused it to an extent that you do whatever you please as there is no accountability. Just imagine a country where you have freedom and cleanliness. Don't you think you would be proud and happy?'

Sid was quiet.

'Let the country not be observed by cameras and as always be monitored by God.'

Sid thought about it deeply.

'I understand, but please . . . think about it,' Sid said haltingly.

Dhootji seemed to read his mind. He thought for a moment.

'All right, let me put it this way. What if the plastic bags no longer existed? I mean, only the carry bags, how is that?' *Dhootji* said, smiling.

Sid was relieved. He found this suggestion interesting and at the same time amusing. The thought of not having a plastic bag to use made him wonder at the consequences.

He was afraid but strangely excited. He chuckled at the thought. After a few minutes of faltering, he said, 'Come on, buddy, let us do this.'

Dhootji nodded and lifted his hand and said, 'From now on, India will be free of plastic bags.'

'Cool,' Sid said, smiling.

CHAPTER SEVEN

The evening was turning dark. Office-goers were returning home. They were anxious to get away from the hustle bustle of the city and reach their peaceful abode called home.

Vegetable sellers were screaming their gut out claiming to be the cheapest. Malls were full of people – some being regular mall-goers, a few people idling their time, salesman just to cool themselves before they would head back on streets selling products, and one or two first timers looking around in awe. All unaware something somewhere was going to change for good.

Raghu, a vegetable vendor, took his usual place and spread out the vegetables. It was business, as usual, for him. He sat in this place for almost eleven years now. He was a migrant who had come to Mumbai to earn his livelihood. But as time passed by, this place was more like home. He lived alone as he could not afford to bring his family. They lived in a remote village in Bihar.

'Boni' or the first customer was very important for any business as it sort of gave a small peek into how the day's business would be. Superstitious it might sound but every businessman, small or big, believed this.

Soon, there was a woman asking for *Bindi* and *masala*, which meant a combination of green chillies, coriander, and ginger.

'*Bhaiya,* put the *masala* in a separate plastic bag. I don't want them to get mixed,' she said arrogantly.

Raghu nodded, thinking these people were so greedy. We were not allowed to use plastic bags and here was this supposedly educated woman asking for two.

Having weighed, he looked around for the plastic bag to put it into. He looked everywhere, but it was not to be found. Cursing, he thought, *Maybe I must have forgotten to bring it along.*

He looked up to the lady and apologised.

'Why don't you check again behind the basket,' the lady said, pointing at a basket behind Raghu.

When Raghu did not find one, she sheepishly removed a cloth bag.

'*Madamji,* if you were carrying a bag, why did you ask for plastic bag?' Raghu asked.

'You just do your work. Who are you to question me?' the woman replied high-handedly.

'*Madamji,* actually, we are not allowed to use them, but we do as we have no choice because people like you insist.'

The woman was silent, clearly not bothered.

As she left, he said, waiting for his next customer, 'God! I forgot the plastic bags at home. What will I do now?'

Meanwhile, somewhere in a mall in the suburbs of Mumbai, there was an unending queue. People were cursing and saying, 'What is going on? What is taking these people so long?'

'What type of service is being rendered to us?' asked some restless customer.

One of them who was standing way behind remarked loudly, 'Is this the way you serve the customers? I will complain to the higher authorities.'

Another person from the queue said, 'It seems the plastic bags from all the counters are missing.'

'Let them get it from their storeroom,' remarked another.

The person cursed loudly. People grew impatient by the minute. Some of them seemed to agree with him. Others were coming up with new ideas.

Meanwhile, the person in the counter returned. Shaking his head, he apologised to the customers and said that the bags were missing from the storeroom too. There was a huge uproar. A media guy among them called a media house and informed them about the missing plastic bags in this particular mall in suburban Mumbai.

No sooner had this person disconnected the phone, a well-known channel aired this incident. A reporter was speaking in a high-pitched voice.

'Breaking news . . . . . . a mysterious case of missing plastic carry bags in a suburban mall in Mumbai' was displayed in white foreground and red background.

Seated in the lavish and comfortably decorated living room in Sid's home, Sid and *Dhootji* were watching breaking news in television.

'So they have caught the wind. I must say these guys are commendable,' *Dhootji* said, smiling.

Meanwhile, the ever-excited reporter continued, 'We have more breaking news coming in. Let us go to our reporter who is reporting live from the announcement desk. What do you have for us, Rohit?' he asked.

Rohit was reporting from a mall, and a huge commotion could be seen behind him.

'We have the store manager here with us, Mr Virani.'

Mr Virani was now an important figure. He appeared a little uneasy. It was his first time on television. He smiled and nodded towards the camera.

'Tell us how did all this happen?' asked a reporter.

'My boys were, as usual, doing the billing process. One of the counters reported that the plastic bags had just vanished. Initially, it was from one counter and later from all of them.'

'What happened later?'

'Some of our customers who had carried cloth bags were asked to come forward and get their billing done so as to avoid a huge crowd.'

'You mean to say the bags that seemed to have vanished were plastic not the cloth bags, right?' confirmed the reporter.

'Yes, then we checked our storeroom where we have a pile of them.'

'And it was not there,' said the reporter, finishing it for him.

'We are sorry for all the inconvenience it has caused our customers. We promise to sort out the matter soon,' said the manager apologising.

'Since five in the evening, there have been reports, and now it is more or less confirmed that plastic bags are not to be found in many parts of Mumbai. We asked several people, and they say they were carrying one, and suddenly, it seemed to have vanished into thin air,' said the reporter, concluding his little revelation.

Dhootji and Sid looked at each other with a smile.

'I am beginning to enjoy this,' Sid said.

'I bet you have.'

There were short interviews showing how a person's now a very worthy possession 'plastic carry bag' had disappeared.

Sid felt thirsty, but he did not want to miss the action, so he remained seated. Reading his thoughts, *Dhootji* handed over a glass of water to Sid from nowhere.

'*Dhootji,* you are so cool really,' Sid said, giving him a thumbs up sign.

By now the news had reached almost all the news channels. Each one tried to outdo the other.

'What do you think could be the reason? Political rip-off? Sting operation or maybe some kind of a scam?' a reporter asked.

'Do let us know. To win a gift voucher from some XYZ company, SMS your answer to the following number,' the reporter said.

The phone number was displayed below, bold and blinking.

Another channel had got four experts into the news studio to speak upon this issue. They discussed legal implications if the person or a party behind this was caught. They seemed to be unsure on the quantum of punishment though.

Sid was now rolling on the floor laughing, saying, 'This is getting even better.'

'How do these guys arrange all this in such a short notice?' wondered *Dhootji*. Shaking his head, he said 'Human mind is fascinating.'

Sid was having a 'time of his life'. All these years, he had been working tirelessly. He never had the time to loosen his tie, and this for sure was a welcome break. Something he really needed.

Meanwhile, a politician promised an unbiased probe into the matter. Another politician talked about handing over the investigation to CBI. Over a period of time, things started settling down.

Soon, people got used to the idea of carrying the cloth bags.

One of the days, Nitya was preparing breakfast in the kitchen.

'*Saab*, do you have any old bed sheets?' she asked.

'Yes, must be in the storeroom. Why do you ask?' said Sid surprised.

'Saab, there is a lot of demand for cloth bags, you know, with plastic bags unavailable. So I thought during my free time I could sew some and sell. May I take a few?'

Sid smiled. Shrewd were those who could turn even a dire situation into their advantage.

'Sure.'

Suddenly, the seemingly insignificant cloth bag's status was elevated to that of a very important commodity. Slowly, things fell into normalcy and people became accustomed to it.

The following morning, Sid left for the hospital for the follow-up. The pain in his back had ceased to exist. He waited outside the consulting room along with a few other patients. From a distance, he saw her. Suddenly, he froze. His heart almost stopped beating.

Wearing a white *salwar kameez* and a shocking pink *leheriya duppata,* Dr Naina walked towards the consulting room. As she walked, a gentle breeze seemed to caress her face; she tried to move a strand of her straightened hair, which seemed to love her cheeks. *Dhootji* was right; she looked like a model sashaying on a ramp. Sid found her much more beautiful than in the pic he had. She was prettier, taller, and slimmer.

Sid was completely taken over by her for a moment. He kept looking at her. Suddenly, he realised the consequences if he stayed on. Not knowing what to do, he prepared to leave.

From a distance, Naina saw Sid getting up. She walked towards him and smiled.

Wow, man, that could kill an army! he thought.

'Where are you going? Your check-up is due.'

Sid looked unsure.

'Wait here. I will see you in a few minutes,' said Naina firmly.

He stopped meekly. He nodded his head sheepishly and sat back waiting. Presently, he was called in. He slowly walked into the consulting room.

Naina smiled and motioned him to be seated.

'How is the pain now?' were the first words from Naina.

Sid was extremely uncomfortable but managed, 'Better.'

'This is awkward,' Sid mumbled.

Naina heard it but chose to ignore it.

'The other day you were in real pain. Good, your friend brought you here on time,' she said with concern.

'You treated me, huh . . . Thank God I am alive,' a surprised Sid blurted out.

'What do you mean? I am thoroughly professional. Personally, I have no complaints. But it is quite surprising that with so many doctors in Mumbai, you had to be treated by me,' she said and chuckled.

'So we are good, right? I mean, I refused to meet you, and I felt it must have hurt you.'

'Oh, certainly, no, it is nice that you have been frank about your relationship, so it is fine by me. I think I like your honesty.'

Sid looked at her tongue-tied.

'You do?' he replied slowly still unable to take his eyes of her. An invisible thread seemed to be pulling him towards her.

What the hell is wrong with me? I am making fool of myself. Dumbass, thought Sid, trying hard to look elsewhere.

'Yes, of course. I mean, both you guys have a great job and are from a similar background. She would be able to understand you better. It is better than making a mistake. I am happy for you.'

She looked more and more beautiful as she spoke. Seeing him staring at her, she was amazed. She wrote down a prescription for a couple of days and handed it over to him.

Sid gathered his lost composure. He took the prescription from her and prepared to leave. He walked towards the door and moved the door handle and instinctively looked up at her.

'Mistake, huh, it is,'

Sid paused, not knowing how to continue, and making an effort, he continued.

'Right now I have lost my job and been dumped by my girlfriend.'

Now it was Naina's turn to stare after him. He smiled, leaving behind a bewildered Naina.

Sid left the hospital. Though the place was full of sick people, it looked more like a sea-facing resort. His heart raced with excitement. He knew he was in love.

CHAPTER EIGHT

It was 5 a.m. Sid was fast asleep. It was dark outside. The October warmth was slowly disappearing and welcoming the little chills of soon-to-be November.

Sid was awoken by a voice which said, 'Time to wake up, Son.'

It was ten days since the first boon. *Dhootji* had arrived for the second.

Sid shifted slowly in his bed. Hearing *Dhootji's* voice, he got up.

'What are you doing here so early?' Sid questioned rubbing his eyes, clearly not wanting to be disturbed.

'Wake up from your dreams, Sid. We have to discuss important matters,' *Dhootji* said firmly.

Sid unwillingly got out of his bed. He freshened up with a cup of coffee in his hand and headed towards the balcony.

Sid offered him a chair, and *Dhootji* sat comfortably.

'I can't believe ten days have gone by,' said Sid.

'Yes, just look at you. You seem to be smiling a lot these days.'

'Nothing, *Dhootji*. It is a beautiful morning. I can hear birds sing too,' Sid said, gesturing his hand high up in the air dramatically.

'Morning was always beautiful, Son. But of course, love makes everything better.'

Sid's face turned beet red. He was unable to contain a silly smile.

'Yes, I guess,' he admitted.

'I am glad,' *Dhootji* said.

'*Dhootji*, I don't know. I mean, how I could not see this earlier.'

'Time, Son, it is just the right time.'

'Hmm.'

'Now that you have a right companion and your second boon is granted, shall we move to the boon-return business?'

'How can you be sure?' Sid asked looking uncertain.

'You mean you are not sure?'

'Of course, I am sure. It is just that she may be seeing someone. Also with my current employment situation, I don't think she would be interested.'

'Love is beyond everything, Son. If it is true, then it has got nothing to do with your employment or looks. A little adjustment here and there will take you both a long way. What is required is the desire to be with the person. If it is there, you will definitely find a way out to be with each other. Moreover, wooing her is your job.

'You mean to say I have to just go there and pop the question?'

'Indeed, Son, do it and do it soon.'

Sid let out a sigh of relief.

'That means she is single. Oh, wow! Thank you. You have taken whole lot of a burden off me. You sure have a way of putting things across.'

Dhootji smiled mischievously. Sid was back in his world with Naina, thinking of different ways to woo her.

'Come back to reality, Son. We have work to do,' *Dhootji* said, snapping his fingers and bringing Sid out of his momentary daydream.

'Oh yes, now that you have given me Naina, what is it that you want in return?' Sid said enthusiastically.

'Disappearance of plastic bags have just worked fine, right?'

'Yes, just fine. I had my doubts though. But it worked wonderfully.'

'So the least we would have landfills clear of plastic bags.'

'Yes, I am happy that I was a part of it.'

'Well, let us get on with the second-boon return.'

'Sure.'

Dhootji cleared his throat and appeared grim.

'The next one is not going to be easy, Sid. But I have to do this,' he said.

Sid looked at *Dhootji* enquiringly. He had just dealt with the first boon. He hoped the second to be easier than the first.

'What do you have in mind? How bad is it, *Dhootji*?' Sid asked a little anxiously.

Dhootji wanted to ease into the subject.

'Well, Son, you have slowly moved towards a life controlled by gizmos. They are paving a way to a generation that would be rendered useless without them. Substantial amount of resources is allotted for tiniest of the tiny organism. The human greed in race towards the improvisation of his lifestyle has grabbed the share of resources that does not belong to him. It is time you put a speed limit to this.'

'What do we do, *Dhootji?* There has been a sharp rise in the population in the recent years. We need to cater to them. They need to survive, right?'

'No, it is not only that. You for your own selfish needs have exploited nature to an extent that you have made a mess of the balance in the ecosystem. You have questioned the very harmony required for the existence of every single organism. "Survival" is the word you use to instantly find justification and excuse for all your transgressions, 'said *Dhootji* in more serious tone.

'Yes,' said Sid, hanging his head in shame.

'What if this happened to you?'

'Huh?'

'Let us get to the bottom of the pile. You get things done at your fingertips. Also, you maintain this so-called balance in your life via gizmos, gadgets, and communication, right?'

'True.'

'What would happen if this communication network was brought down?'

'The backbone of the entire society as a whole would collapse.'

'Exactly, and that is the reason I want to take away the very foundation of communication.'

'Huh?'

'The Internet.'

Sid looked at *Dhootji* questioningly.

'Pardon.'

'You heard me right, Son, network of networks the Internet.'

'But why? Good lord, why the Internet . . . huh . . . ? What are you trying to prove anyway?' Sid stammered.

The words coming from *Dhootji* were sharp. It took him some time to sink in. When it did, it made him extremely uneasy.

'Oh yes, I was expecting this question. Internet is considered to be the cyber equivalent of an ecosystem. Let me see what you would do if I pull the plug on your ecosystem.'

'But, *Dhootji,* Internet and the new form of communication has helped us save trees.'

'Of course, but do you realise that not using paper does not mean you are moving towards a greener planet. On the contrary, every single byte of storage or a simple search has its impact on environment in the form of energy consumption, which later transforms itself to carbon emissions.'

Sid took in the information startled. He had never heard of this before or never bothered about it. It reminded him of his boss at Ascii Solutions, Mr Jignesh Mehta. He was called the '*Kanjoos* Mehta' or '*Gaass puuss*

Man', not for being vegetarian but for his efforts in making the office green.

A true nature lover, he had all the old bulbs in his office and home replaced by the LED bulbs. He encouraged his team into the habit of switching everything off at the end of the day and implement energy-saving modes. He had strict instructions given to his axillary staff to make sure that office lights, air conditioning, and microwaves were turned off fully at the end of the day. He kept his mailbox in order by deleting unwanted mails and unsubscribing newsletters that he was not interested in any more.

Sid took a deep breath.

'The energy consumed and the carbon footprints left behind by usage of net is extremely high,' observed *Dhootji.*

'But, *Dhootji,* we cannot resort to another form of communication now. Maybe if people are made aware, we may do so over the years.'

'It is too late, Son.'

Sid heaved a sigh.

What is going to happen? he thought.

World Wide Web was a part of each individual's life, rich or poor. Sid had always been amazed at the mammoth tasks an Internet could do. Everything from presentations to communication was made extremely easy. Time was never a constraint now. With a few clicks here and there, things would get going. It was a huge boon for a population like ours. The thought of not having net facility for ticket booking or money transfer was chaotic.

Imagine a day without ATM machine, Sid wondered.

He remembered the days when he would accompany his grandpa to a bank where money transfer would lead him to series of counters with a never-ending queue in each. With the kind of population now, it was unthinkable.

As a child, he would wait for his grandfather's cards for his birthday. Though he knew he would never forget his only grandchild's birthday, a day late would make him restless. He had made penfriends whom he had written to till he was in teens and later lost touch. But the excitement of buying card, posting the letter, or getting one from them those days was something he would look forward to. Now birthday cards were replaced by e-card. Actually, most of the things were replaced by e and a hyphen.

Sid's first computer was gifted to him by his father on his tenth birthday. He had proudly shown his Pentium to his friends who would have been thankful even if they would receive a 486 for their birthdays. But yes, of course, now these words sounded ancient.

Somewhere in 90s, an engineer irrespective of his branch would take up a computer course from various computer institutes, which had mushroomed in every city, and head for the United States.

Soon, the typing and shorthand courses were replaced by computer courses. In no time, India and in particular Bangalore and Hyderabad became the highest supplier of a newly coined term called the 'software engineers' to the world. Of course, it gave the Indian economy a much-needed boost.

Krishna Kumar, one of Sid's batchmate, was one such engineer. His father was a fruit seller. He got into his school through scholarship. Being a good student all along, he completed his Engineering in Mining through a quota and had later completed his computer course from a reputed institute. Soon, a job offer followed, and he was sent to Los Angeles for a project.

Of course, this was a huge deal for families coming from a not-so-wealthy background and had never travelled or seen places. Gone were the days when only a few rich went abroad.

Now with the software boom, even a poor but an educated engineer like Krishna Kumar could afford to send visa to his parents. His parents had never stepped outside their state let alone abroad or had been through a journey by an aeroplane. Soon, pictures of Krishna Kumar's parents taken in Universal Studio, Disneyland, and even Las Vegas were seen. Thanks to social networking sites!

With the advent of Internet and smartphone apps, there was seldom a need for Sid to step out of his home for shopping. It had made his life much simpler. He had brought cloths, books, groceries, and even vegetables online. It had saved his time. There was buy-back, cashback, and many other back-to-back schemes, and Sid never complained.

Sid's grandfather, who was in his late eighties, lived with his parents in Chandigarh. He loved his grandfather immeasurably, who also happened to be a fitness freak. Sid would order shoes, tracksuit, and many other things for him online, which would be delivered in straight forty-eight hours. It also had the much-needed exchange facility.

He had wondered the day his trash collector Raju had rung his bell and as Sid kept his trash can out, he was surprised to see Raju holding a nice big smartphone and laughing at some joke passed on to him.

Seeing Sid, he had told, '*Saab,* shall I send it to you,' with sparkle in his eyes.

Truly, India with the kind of population was in for a race for highest cellphone users.

Sid remembered when he was young, he would accompany his parents to a restaurant. There would be many others like them, out with their family talking, laughing, and generally having a great time. But now when he would walk into a coffee shop, it would be quiet like an examination hall.

With one person at every table texting continuously, the fun of eating out was no longer there.

It was a sad sight when you did not have anyone to share with other than a virtual world that hardly cared.

With the social networking services, he had once again connected to his long-lost classmates and cousins who stayed abroad. He had also made a few new friends on these sites. It was a great platform for introverts to make friends, for the *Bahus* to outdo each other as there were more and more nuclear families, and this was the only way to keep up in touch. Blogging new ideas was a trend which people from creative field followed.

Business now was completely online. A not-so-learned person could start a business online with companies offering domains free of cost. It made business look not only cool but also savvy. It was a win, win situation for all.

Heaving a sigh, Sid came to the present.

'*Dhootji*, this is simply outrageous. People will not be able to survive without the Internet.'

'Your reaction for plastic was similar. Look, how well people have adapted to the change.'

'Please do not compare the two. They are not alike.'

'Yes, they are. Maybe a little more adjustment is needed.'

'I know of companies which have taken steps to use 100 per cent renewable energy.'

'Yes, I know the greening of Internet happening,' said *Dhootji* unmoved.

'Think about it, *Dhootji*. It has this immense data, business connectivity, and God, I just can't think any more. It has become so part of each one's life. It is simply not possible to do away with it. Please ask for something else.'

'The decision is not mine. After all your survival instincts are so strong that you will find a way out. So let me see how you handle this.'

'But, *Dhootji,* this is a near-to-death situation.'

'No, Son, the near-to-death situation is yet to come. This is just the second boon.'

Sid stared at *Dhootji. Was this worth pursuing?* he wondered. He felt like he was standing on a burning deck.

Dhootji looked at him and tried to convince him. But Sid shook his head in disagreement.

'Let us forget the Internet for some time,' said *Dhootji* in deep thought.

'So you do have a choice,' said Sid accusingly.

'Actually, very little. I do have a better alternative though,' said *Dhootji,* unable to contain a smile.

What was better now? Sid wondered.

'This is not funny, *Dhootji.*'

'Well, let me make it a little easier. How about say smartphone? Smartphone, yes, that is it.'

'Oh, please, *Dhootji,* people may forget to wear cloths but will never forget to carry their smartphone,' Sid said gloomily.

'No, I am talking about the apps in it.'

'What about them?'

'What if the apps from the smartphone disappeared?'

'Oh, . . . you mean the smartphone which we use now will function only as a phone of say 90s?'

Sid was doubtful. He himself could not think of a day without smartphone. It was like saying 'of two evils choose the less', either Internet or apps.

Dhootji knew of Sid's confusion.

'Do not push this further, Son. Trust me, it is not going to be that bad as you make it to be.'

Sid was not sure, but he had to honour the commitment. Somehow the trust he had laid on *Dhootji* seemed to assure him, and also, he did not have an alternative.

Sid nodded his approval reluctantly.

Dhootji chuckled and declared to Sid's annoyance.

'From now on smartphone will no longer be smart.'

Sid sat down helplessly as *Dhootji* vanished.

CHAPTER NINE

It was a bright morning. Ishika, a grade 10 student, was woken up by the alarm sound. After five snoozes, she decided to wake up. First thing she reached out for was the smartphone. She tried to check the messages. The screen was blank.

Shucks! I forgot to put it on charge, she thought.

Switching on the charger, she promptly went back to sleep. Thousands of Ishika's out there seemed to be doing the same thing right now.

In Delhi, Mr Arora's home was bustling with activity as their only daughter, Richa, was to be getting married in a fortnight. There were many ceremonies including *mehendi, sangeet, tilak,* to name a few. The Arora's had planned their entire wedding shopping online, and today being an auspicious day, they were ready for online shopping. They needed outfits for every occasion. It had to match with the theme. Their net-savvy daughter Richa and the family gathered in the living room. Richa had already zeroed in on three happening online shopping web sites for her wedding ensemble for various occasions.

Aunts, uncles, and cousins moved forward to have a close look at her shopping cart. Richa had turned on her tab for the third time; somehow she had trouble getting the apps on the screen. Cursing, she restarted the tab for the fourth time. She finally called her bestie Natasha to check.

Richa and Natasha were close friends and part of around twenty groups on a messenger. Each group had a minimum of 200 participants. Each time they shared a joke, pics, or video clips, it was circulated to all the participants. Out of them, only maybe 30 per cent actually read them. Initially, it was all fun as the number of groups and the number of participants were less. They would wait eagerly for a message and read them with enthusiasm. Later, it became repetitive and annoying. Now they would check messages of those groups that actually mattered. Unknown to them, somewhere every repetitive or unread message left behind a digital footprint.

'OMG, I know. It is like ages. I am going crazy. I mean come on *yaar.* I have not checked my messages since morning, dude. I mean like four hours. How gross is that?' said her friend who sounded deeply cross.

It looked like the message she was supposed to have received was to save the mankind from some crisis not too far.

After comforting her, Richa disconnected the phone. An impatient uncle got up.

'I told you to have a look at Sukhram's store. He has everything from garlands to dresses all stocked up at one place. How could you listen to these kids? As it is they are so lazy. They don't want to step out of the house. They want everything home delivered. It is time they listen to the elders.'

He looked at the twins who were Richa's cousins from Jalander.

'Look at these two. Since they have come here, they have not stepped out of the house, eating pizza and playing video games. Look, how obese they have become.'

The twins looked at him piercingly.

'Don't look at me like that. At your age, we would help our elders . . .' Before he could complete the sentence, one of them stopped him.

'*Thavuji,* we don't want to know what you did. This is the Yoyo- gen. Stop lecturing us.'

'Sure, you don't want to listen to anyone. The cloths you are wearing and the hairstyle. God! I fail to understand.'

'*Thavuji,* this is called being in vogue. You will never understand,' said one of the twins, laughing.

Richa, who was listening to this, smiled. Her tab still failed to bring the apps to life.

'Just calm down, *Thavuji.* I will take care of everything. The problem will be solved soon. Probably, the signal is weak. It happens all the time.'

Thavuji was in no mood to relent.

'*Beta,* we don't have that kind of time. If we see Sukhramji and place the order today, maybe we will get things on time.'

An anxious Arora family collectively agreed. There were nods of agreement from the elders, whereas kids did not want to go out in the sun and preferred a comfortable shopping from home.

There were so many families out there where this scene being played but maybe a little differently. Little did they know that every order they placed emitted a few grams of carbon.

Somewhere down south in Kerala, Mr Pillai was beginning his daily morning ritual of checking his daughter's profile on a match-finding site and looking for any prospective groom. His daughter was a software engineer working at LA, USA. He wanted her to settle down with an NRI. He had already rejected five proposals. Not finding a suitable groom from his community, he had decided to go groom hunting online at his friend's behest.

Today, he was a little upset that the apps on his phone were not working. Further annoyed, he tried restarting the phone, a probable solution his daughter had suggested.

Well, something was wrong. He picked up the newspaper and forgot about the app for the time being. There were thousands of Pillais out there doing the same right now. If only he had known that every profile he checked lessened the amount of oxygen for the soon-to-be-born babies.

Somewhere in coastal Karnataka, an eco-friendly Mr Bhat had stopped bringing newspaper as a campaign to save trees. He believed in greener India. He read the newspaper online. His morning would begin with thirty minutes of yoga and later go through all the news apps.

Today was different. His tablet screen was totally blank. His tablet was still under warranty. He decided to visit the nearest showroom.

Maybe I could get it repaired or replaced, he thought. He connected his tab to a charger and went back to preparing tea.

There was thousands of Bhats doing this right now. If only he realised that the saved trees have to sequester more carbon emissions to stabilise the atmosphere.

In the most happening city Mumbai, Apoorv Chopra got up early morning for his early morning workout. He belonged to a wealthy Punjabi industrialist family. They lived in Juhu. He was seventeen years of age and a gifted cricketer.

He had recently recovered from a ligament tear, and his doctor had forbid him from undergoing any kind of physical training in the gym. Instead, the doctor said that light jogging in open air would be the best form of exercise and would help him recover soon.

His training app helped him create a workout schedule. It was easy to use. It was accurate. It maintained a run log that composed of distance and time he walked. It let him set goals for himself. Apoorv was a very hard-working boy despite the fact that he came from an extremely wealthy family. His goal was to somehow make it to the IPL cricket team next year.

He would wake up early in the morning and head towards Aarey Colony. This was one green patch of

Mumbai that supplied oxygen to the entire city. He loved the greenery and the smell of fresh air.

It was quite deserted in the morning. His driver dropped him at the Aarey tollbooth and went away to have his morning *chai* from a nearby *Chaiwala*. Apoorv got down from the car and put on his headphones. He played the music of his choice. As he walked slowly, he tried turning on his fitness app. It did not open. He tried again in vain.

There were many more fitness freaks doing the same in every corner of the country. Each time they checked their fitness stats, it reduced the fitness of their planet.

It was afternoon with apps still not working, Richa and the entire family set out to Sukhramji's shop. They were welcomed with smiles and juice to drink. The bride was given extra attention. Various fabrics that Richa had never known existed were shown. She particularly liked a tomato red colour one. She went on to choose the design and pattern. Once the bride trousseau was done, it was the turn of various aunts and cousins. Each outfit selected had to go through Richa's approval. One of the cousins protested for which Sukhramji politely said, 'It's *Babyji's shaadi* so she should be the one who decides.'

Richa enjoyed the attention and felt the wedding jitters for the first time. After thanking Sukhramji, one of the aunts suggested a *chaat* outlet. So the family hogged on the *chaat* and *lassi* and headed home satisfied.

Nitya came over in an unusually dull mood. Sid had never seen her like this.

'Nitya, what happened? Are you unwell?'

'No, *Saab*, just a little sad.'

'What happened?'

'Nothing, *Saab*, we maids from this building have a group on messaging app. We send jokes to each other. I normally read three to four jokes every morning before I come to work. Today, I don't know why I have not received a single message.'

Sid kept staring after her.

By now most of the service providers and companies who had their app up there were bombarded with customer complaints. There was a huge data block. Grievances kept piling every minute. The pending orders, undelivered stock, and the lack of tracking system led to a total mess.

Companies abroad began to panic. They had heard about the mysterious disappearance of plastic bags. They did not find any reason to link the two. But both were sort of eerie.

The call centres were struggling and trying to keep calm and at the same time were giving the usual reason for this unusual situation.

'There is a minor problem with the server, sir, will bounce back in no time,' Shilpa said, trying to sound as casual as possible.

'Server is on a regular maintenance and would be up very soon,' Shilpa said to another caller.

'Your money would be transferred soon, sir. Meanwhile, why don't you go through the process again via our web site,' Shilpa said to yet another caller.

'Is that working?'

'Yes, sir,' Shilpa said.

Thank God for that, she thought.

This was her maybe thousandth caller. She had lost count.

'I am tired of doing this shit,' said Shilpa, throwing away the headphones.

'Shilpa, hang on, there is another caller. I know this sucks, but we need to go on,' said a voice next to her.

It was Megha. She too, like Shilpa, was tired of answering the calls. It was a busy day.

All the call centres showed the similar signs of desperation and exhaustion.

We are an extremely adaptable species . Unknown to us our mind comes up with a plan B and in no time finds a way out even if the solution is temporary.

It was four in the evening, and ten-year-old Kush came home from the school. As usual, he was accompanied by his maid from the bus stop. Once home, Kush throwing his bag went to the bedroom to collect his tab. He loved to play online games. The maid at the background kept yelling, 'Kush Baba, first freshen up, have snacks, and then go to play.'

Kush pretended not to hear her and continued restarting his tablet for the second time. Apparently, it was still not working. He called up his friend Adu, who in turn called another friend Rahul.

Maid sensed something was wrong as she had never seen Kush so upset.

'Kush Baba, what happened? Did you forget to take down your homework?'

Kush looked at her. 'I have forgotten so many times. Did I ever call up anyone?' Kush replied dryly.

'Then?' asked the maid.

Kush looked at his tablet.

'This damn thing is not working.'

'Oh, is that all.'

Kush looked at her coldly. His virtual goal was to unlock a mystery, get some gold, and move up at least five levels for a day in an online game. Gone were those days when kids were taught to have realistic goals. The parents themselves were busy out there in the virtual world where the fight was on to prove their mere existence in this domain.

'This is so gross,' Kush said, throwing away the tablet on the sofa.

At around six in the evening, Kush and his friends decided to meet up in their apartment play area.

Late in the evening, when Kush's parents arrived from the work, an enthusiastic Kush told his parents about his game of basketball with his friends and how much he had enjoyed playing with them.

'You know, Papa, impressed by my game, they made me the captain of the team. I am looking forward for the following day's play,' said an excited Kush.

His parents looked at each other. They had never seen their son so happy.

In the excitement, Kush forgot to tell them about the online games. He had his dinner without fuss, and a tired Kush slept soundly.

Little did he know that each time he went a level ahead in his online game, planet Earth went a level ahead in global warming.

As usual, the story of the disappeared apps made its way to the television.

There were analysis, discussions, and accusations. The connection between the disappearance of plastic bags and apps was quite evident, but 'what was it?' was something they were currently exploring. The excitement waned away slowly.

Sid was no longer interested in it, maybe because he was hardly using it these days. He watched the headlines where every channel had something or the other to say. He remembered what he had to say to Naina and made his way to the hospital the following day.

CHAPTER TEN

Sid was unable to sleep. He kept rehearsing his act of proposal for the umpteenth time. Strangely, he felt more nervous each time. He thought of carrying a bunch of flowers. *Maybe she will throw it at me. That will be embarrassing.* He skipped the idea. *What about a box of chocolates?*

Women no matter how old always liked them. It was their idea of romance. *She can throw that too,* he thought.

After giving it a thought, he decided to clear things first. Then maybe flowers or chocolates would help.

He carefully dressed in a well-fitted denims and a comfortable blue linen shirt.

Naina was already there and so were the patients, waiting to see her. As Sid's turn arrived, he felt like a teenager in love. As he sat down, he noticed she looked more beautiful.

'How are you? How is the pain?' she asked.

'Doctor, back doesn't hurt any more, but there is this fierce pain in my heart which refuses to go unless you have coffee with me,' Sid replied nervously.

She moved forward and looked into his eyes angrily.

'What do you think you are doing? Are you flirting with me?'

Their eyes lingered for a second.

Sid unknowingly got up from the chair and moved towards her. In one single move, he turned her chair. He noticed she looked even more beautiful in a white kurta and blue denims. Naina stared after him and slowly managed to say, 'Are you crazy?'

Sid ignored her and moved closer. He held her hand and went down on his knees.

'Look, Doctor, I have no clue what I am doing. Please say yes before this patient of yours suffers a stroke.'

It took a couple of seconds for Naina to regain her lost composure. Then a smile broke all over her gentle face.

'Oh, all right, maybe sometime next week,' she said and chuckled.

Sid opened his eyes widely.

'Are you planning to kill me slowly?'

Naina could not help but laugh.

'You are impossible.'

She paused not knowing what to say. She thought for a moment and looked at him curiously.

'Fine, let me see maybe tomorrow evening at the coffee shop near the hospital.'

Sid let out a sigh of relief.

'That's better. You have saved a life today.'

Naina smiled.

'Now, please leave I have work to do,' she said.

Sid nodded and gave her one last glance. As he left the hospital, he felt he was the happiest man alive.

The following day, Sid kept checking his watch every now and then. A surge of pleasure ran through him as the afternoon approached.

He heard a voice that said, 'Waiting for the evening?'

Sid turned around to see *Dhootji*. He smiled.

'Can't you cut short the day, *Dhootji*?'

'You are always impatient. There is so much happiness in waiting,' *Dhootji* replied.

As the evening approached, Sid dressed up in beige stretchable cotton chinos and white shirt, which he had kept for special occasions. He put on a splash of the perfume which was priced at thousands for a drop.

'You look like a prince. Now go charm your princess,' *Dhootji* said, giving Sid a thumbs up sign and signing off.

Sid drove happily and reached much before the chosen time. He enjoyed looking at Naina walking towards him. She wore plain green dress with earrings to match. He pulled out the chair for her. She sat down thanking him.

The evening went on very well. Other than their professions, they had almost everything in common from sports to travel destinations, books to choice of movies and music.

There was a time when Naina spoke about the disappearance of plastic bags and the apps.

'First, plastic bags now apps, this is something weird, right?' Naina said.

'Yes.' Sid nodded, trying not to give away anything.

'Do you think it is some kind of a scam? I mean, how could something like this happen?' Naina asked.

Sid was a little uncomfortable.

'I don't know. I have not given it much of a thought as I am currently busy thinking of you,' Sid said, trying to change the topic that was making him uneasy.

Naina ignored him.

'Plastic bags, I think, are gone for good, but apps are very useful, don't you think?' Naina asked.

Happy that Naina was in agreement with him over the first boon, he somehow changed the topic.

Both had so much to talk to each other that they never realised how the time flew by until the waiter informed them about the closing.

Sid dropped Naina at home, and she promised to meet him soon. As both reached home, they missed each other immensely.

In all the excitement, the act of the disappearing apps seemed to have taken a backseat. Sid no longer watched the news to hear the latest updates.

He spent most of the time dreaming and planning his future with Naina. He would wait for the evening when Naina would make some time for him. Being a visiting doctor in three hospitals, Naina had a hectic schedule shuffling between the hospitals.

Sid cherished this moment and looked forward for this little time every evening he spent with her.

It was Saturday evening, Amit, Naina's brother, had completed his work a little early. He decided to pick up Naina. He thought of calling her first but decided to surprise her. He reached the hospital and was looking around for parking place. He found one towards his left. As soon as he made his way towards it, he saw Naina with a guy.

He happened to be familiar. He tried to remember but was unable to place him. Both were holding hands and looked at each other fondly. They got into a car that was parked diagonally opposite Amit's car.

Soon, he knew who he was. He could simply knock this guy off but resisted. He watched the car pass by. He drove back home and waited. Amit was four years older than Naina. He was extremely protective about her. They were very close to each other. When his parents had told him about Sid, he was a little sceptical. After seeing Sid's pic, he was convinced. He found him snobbish. Marrying a complete stranger was a big NO.

Naina had many proposals, but she had not shown interest in any of them. With Sid, it was different. She had agreed to meet him hence he relented. After conveying their interest, they had patiently waited for Sid's response. The wait was quite long, which made Amit furious. After two months, their parents met again in a *satsang* and were informed of Sid seeing someone else and which they too were unaware of. When Amit told Naina of Sid's refusal to meet her, she was a little hurt. But she did not show. She never did.

Late in the evening, Naina came home. Amit noticed the extra glow on her face. He wanted to speak to her regarding this but decided against it. He thought he would handle it differently.

It was Sunday morning when Sid opened the door to a complete stranger. He looked at Sid and said, 'Hello, I am Amit, Amit Soni,' in a deep firm voice.

Sid knew instantly. He could spell 'trouble'.

'May I,' he continued as Sid ushered him to the living room.

He was over six feet with a great personality. He wore denims with red and blue block checks long-sleeved shirt. His eyes glared at Sid. It meant business. Sid was intimidated by his looks. Both sat down.

'Nice house,' he said looking around.

'Thanks,' Sid said.

'I don't suppose you know me.'

'No, I do,' Sid said, not knowing what else to add.

'Sorry, I did not mean to gatecrash like this. But this is important. I am sure you know why I am here,' he said, slowly looking at Sid.

Sid nodded.

'I hate hypocrisy. I hate lies,' Amit said.

Sid heard, 'I hate you. I hate your family.'

Sid looked at Amit with complete attention.

'Look, let me ask you straight. Are you seeing my sister?'

Sid hesitated.

'Yes,' he said finally.

When Amit heard this, the expression of his face began to change.

'Since when?'

This sounded more like being interrogated.

Sid took a deep breath and described his side of story to Amit. His lost job, broken engagement, mishap, being treated by Naina, and finally falling in love with her.

Amit heard him out and actually enjoyed the part when Sid said how he was trying to get away from the hospital after he had spotted Naina.

His smile reminded him of Naina. Both laughed wholeheartedly. Amit's love for his sister was evident.

Suddenly, he appeared serious.

'Oh, great! You don't have a job. Your fiancée has dumped you. Now you are going around with my sister whom you had even refused to meet earlier. How convenient, huh,' Amit said.

'No, no, no, you got me all wrong. It is not like that.'

'To me it definitely looks like that,' he said, shaking his head, trying to understand this.

'I know, with my current situation, you think less of me. But I promise it is going to change soon.'

'How do you purpose to do that?' asked Amit, raising his eyebrow.

Sid thought for a few seconds. He remembered Rishabh telling him about the consultancy. He repeated it to Amit.

'I have contacts and enough start-up money for investing in some new venture.'

'That sounds nice, but will it work in reality?'

'Yes, of course, I am doing the necessary ground work,' Sid said, trying to sound as truthful as possible.

'I am sorry I am being a little rude. May I ask you something?

'Sure, go ahead.'

'This house . . . eh . . . do you own it?'

'Yes, but I have a little loan to pay off.'

'Oh, good to hear. How do you pay your EMIs?'

'I have enough savings.'

'How long will that last?'

'At least for some time.'

'Have you informed your parents about this?'

'About what?'

Amit let out a sigh and said, 'About Naina, of course.'

'No. I am waiting for the right time.'

'Great, and when would that be?'

'Once I set up my business.'

'Look, I don't want to rush. But as a brother, all I ask is I want you to at least get engaged to her.'

'*Bhaiyya*', he paused, 'I love Naina, and I mean it. I know you are a little cross about me not seeing her earlier and now that I have lost everything I am dating her. But even in this situation, if I am the happy, Naina is the reason. Just give me some time, and I am sure I will make up for all this,' Sid said.

His eyes softened.

'Look, Siddarth, I am not cross. Actually, you are very different from what I have pictured of you. Fair enough you are committed. But I don't want my sister to be just a rebound for you being dumped.'

'Of course, not,' Sid said genuinely.

'Fine, I will give you some time. I am not asking you to turn rich overnight. I just want you to earn a decent amount and take good care of my sister.'

'Thanks for understanding. I would never do anything to hurt her.'

'You better not because if you do, I am going to hit you hard where it hurts,' he said getting up.

Sid smiled.

'Also, I don't want my sister to know about this,' he said.

Sid nodded. He asked him for coffee. Amit declined. He wished Sid luck and left.

Sid sat down on the sofa and let out a heavy sigh.

CHAPTER ELEVEN

During one of the conversations with Rishabh, Sid told him about Naina. Rishabh was surprised and happy at the same time. He had already met Naina at the hospital. They decided to meet soon.

Sid was a member of one of the town's esteemed club. He and Rishabh decided to meet there for an elaborate seven-course meal. He called the hotel and made the necessary dinner reservations.

Sid and Naina were picked up by Rishabh and Payal the following evening. Naina was dressed in a Turkish blue dress with white bead work, which enhanced her figure. Payal was in a well-fitted maroon colour skirt with playful layers at the knees and a simple white top. Both looked beautiful. Men chose to wear comfortable semi-formal outfit.

At the hotel, they were received by the hotel staff. As Sid was a frequent visitor, they knew him very well.

They were taken to the seats reserved for them. They sat down comfortably. The place was dimly lit with soft music being played in the background.

As they ordered for drinks, Sid saw a familiar figure at a distance having an intimate conversation with another person. His face turned pale. Soon, the blur figures became clearer.

Seeing Kamya and Yash, his first thought was to leave the place, but he thought better of it.

After a few moments, Kamya saw Sid and was a little mortified. She seemed to be telling Yash about this, who turned around. Naina and Rishabh, who had been seeing Sid staring at another table, turned around too. To Sid's astonishment, Yash waved at Naina. Sid looked at her surprised.

'How do you know that loser?' Sid blurted out.

Rishabh and his wife looked at her too.

'How do you know him?' Naina said coolly.

'He is the one I told you about, the current managing director of Ascii Solutions, and the girl with him is Kamya,' said Sid, letting out a sarcastic smile.

'Oh, great! I was one of the doctors who had treated Yash's father during his knee replacement surgery.'

'Man! This is interesting,' Rishabh said.

'Oh! This is amazing. You should have broken Yash's bones instead,' Sid said angrily.

'I almost did that,' Naina said, laughing.

All the three looked at her wondering.

Over the dinner, they learnt how Naina had met the remarkable Yash.

'His father was admitted in one of the hospitals I work for. I was to assist the doctor in charge. He would bring flowers for his father every day. When I would come for my daily rounds, he would meet me in the pretext of enquiring about his father's health. He would then hand over a rose and ask me out. On the day his father was discharged, he even proposed. My God, he is so dumb,' Naina said.

'He is not dumb but extremely shrewd and calculative,' Sid pointed out.

Rishabh agreed.

'May be, but he has this "I am a flirt" written all over his face. One must be stupid not to see it,' Naina said.

Payal laughed.

'If Kamya is seeing him, I am really sorry for her. She looks nice though,' Naina said without hesitation.

Sid looked at Naina surprised.

He found Naina very easy to be with. She was one of the most secure persons he had met. Given the present scenario, any girl would have freaked out. But Naina was different; she was blessed with ability to handle things effectively and looked perfectly sorted.

They ordered, and rest of the evening went on well. They paid and prepared to leave. Rishabh and Payal went a little ahead to get their car. Sid and Naina waited. After a few minutes, they bumped into Yash and Kamya.

Both were dressed in office wear. *Must have come from the office directly,* thought Sid.

The *thought* of office made him feel sick. By now Kamya knew who Naina was. Sid had mentioned about her when they used to go out.

Yash moved cordially towards them. However annoying he was, he had excellent public manners. He would always ignore any kind of unpleasantness. Even during the time of crisis, he would smile and put up a face that said everything was just remarkable. Sid found this nauseating.

How could someone be so deceptive? he wondered.

They greeted each other. Kamya could not bring herself to meet Sid's eyes. Yash took a pace forward.

'Hello, Dr Naina, delighted to see you,' Yash said looking at Naina as he shook hands with her.

Later, he looked at Sid, Rishabh, and his wife and said, 'Hello.'

Kamya had shared a close friendship with Rishabh and his wife. She was always a part of their so-called group. They had gone together for weekend getaways, dinners, and parties and had bonded very well. Today, seeing some else in her place made her bitter. She said a quick hello to all of them.

There was tension in the air. Other than Naina, everyone seemed to be positioned awkwardly. They tried to mask it by sounding cordial.

'So, Naina, it has been a very long time,' Yash said. Not waiting for her to reply, he continued, admiring Naina, 'You are seeing Sid, I gather. I must say, Sid, you are a very lucky man.'

Sid nodded, and they prepared to leave.

From the corner of his eye, Yash could see both Sid and Kamya in an uneasy situation. He happened to enjoy this.

He continued to chat with Naina, and she in turn enquired about his father.

Meanwhile, Kamya stepped a little closer to Sid.

'Sid, may I have a word with you?'

Sid looked at Naina, who nodded. Rishabh told Sid he would be waiting for them in the car, and after bidding a quick goodbye, he left with his wife.

As they took a few steps ahead, Kamya turned towards Sid.

'How have you been, Sid?'

Sid looked at her. The 'how have you been' seemed more like 'are you alive'.

'To tell you the truth, Kamya, past two months has been great. I have never felt something like this before.'

'She is lovely, Sid. Your mother was right,' Kamya said with complete honesty.

'Oh, that she is. I am happy for you and Yash too,' Sid replied.

Kamya remained silent.

When Sid left the job, Yash had consoled her, and all the time she had known that she never loved Yash and he was just a rebound. Seeing Sid with another girl made her heart ache.

The time spent with Sid was something she was unable to forget. But sadly, all that she could see now was a pair of emotionless eyes. His aloofness hurt her immensely as she had never anticipated this. Suddenly, she lifted her hand.

'Let us remain friends, Sid.'

Sid let out a small laugh.

'That part of my life is far behind me, Kamya. And friend is a word with a very deep meaning. I am sure

I don't want you to be burdened by it. Let us part as acquaintances so that we would be civil just in case we bump into each other again,' Sid said flatly and walked towards Naina, who was still having a conversation with Yash.

There was a vacant look on Sid's face devoid of all emotions as he moved forward. Kamya knew she had lost Sid forever. She felt she was forcefully stabbed with a blunt knife.

Payal signalled from a distance.

Taking Naina by hand, a relieved Sid bid goodbye to Yash and moved towards the car, leaving behind a miserable Kamya staring at them.

It was over, done with, she thought.

It was quite a scene. All of them were unusually quiet on their way back home. Naina was first to be dropped. As Naina got down, Sid and Payal got down too.

Payal turned towards Naina and said, 'I have known Sid and Kamya for a very long time. I found them to be perfect for each other. But having said that, I would always feel there was something missing. Kamya complemented Sid. But you not only complement Sid but you complete him.'

Naina smiled. She thanked and hugged her.

CHAPTER TWELVE

These ten days seemed to have passed quickly. Unknown to Sid, *Dhootji* was sitting by his bedside waiting for him to wake up.

Rubbing his eyes, Sid saw a blur figure. It was *Dhootji*.

'Hi, *Dhootji*,' Sid said, still sleepy and trying to open his eyes.

'Looks like you have forgotten me already,' *Dhootji* said.

Sid hauled out of his bed and said, 'Oh no, it is not like that. I have stopped using sleeping pills altogether. I sleep like a baby now.'

'That is good to hear, Son.'

'I never thought I would be able to give them up. I feel so much at peace.'

'I am glad you did. Now with peace restored, I have come for my last boon.'

Sid was in the kitchen making coffee.

'Yes, of course, it is your turn to ask. But first, let me finish with the coffee.'

He sipped his coffee as *Dhootji* sat down on the cane chair.

'I want to thank you for bringing Naina into my life,' Sid began.

Dhootji smiled.

'I feel I have the strength to face anything, and I know that somewhere you are responsible for this,' he continued.

He narrated his meeting with Kamya and Yash.

Dhootji laughed.

During Sid's earlier encounters with *Dhootji*, he would always be pleasant and relaxed. But today, looking at *Dhootji* made him uneasy. He looked tensed. Something was bothering him. Sid tried not to think of it.

Dhootji moved his lips to speak. His voice was grim.

'Son, time has come for the last takeaway and the most difficult one.'

'Sure, it has.'

To proceed was difficult, to retreat was impossible, thought Sid.

'What is it that you want?'

'I don't know how to put it across.'

Dhootji was unable to meet his eyes. He waited for some time before he spoke.

'But I have no choice. I know this is going to be very tough and maybe even unthinkable. So I want you to be brave and face it like a man.'

'Speak it out, *Dhootji*. I cannot handle this suspense anymore.'

Dhootji took a deep breath and said, 'Very soon, India will be in complete darkness as my third boon would be taking away electricity.'

Sid turned pale, the implications being obvious. He felt as if the ground were slipping beneath his feet.

There was an uncomfortable silence. He looked at *Dhootji* blankly and tried to speak but felt a lump in his throat. He was not prepared for something as huge as this. He looked at *Dhootji* in complete disbelief.

'Electricity, wow! This is totally insane. I mean, I can't think of a life without it. It would be like going back to medieval period with some time machine.'

He closed his eyes and tried not to think of it as if not thinking of the consequences would make *Dhootji* change his mind.

He got up slowly, recovering from the shock.

How are I and my fellow men going to face this cruel reality?

A deadly sickness came over him.

'Do you even hear yourself, *Dhootji*, this is not something I had signed up for,' Sid said.

Not waiting for him to answer, he continued.

'Do you believe that taking away electricity would solve the problems?' Sid wailed.

A long silence followed.

'Son, I have no control over this. I am just a messenger. My duty is to pass on the message,' *Dhootji* said gently.

Sid had read articles time and again that the overuse of natural resources by humans was leading to global warming, deforestation, polluted air and water. The problem was getting worse as population and consumption kept growing, and if nothing changed, mankind would need many more planets in order to sustain the kind of lifestyle they were used to.

'Son, this is not about you, your friends, or your family any more. It is about the entire universe. I know this is difficult, but I am as helpless as you are. Only thing I could do is see that important places like water supplies and transportation would not be affected.'

'I am much relieved to hear it,' he said.

After this, Sid made no further remarks.

Having said so, *Dhootji* simply disappeared as did the electricity. Sid had no idea what he was expected to do or what was going to happen next.

It was 10 a.m. There was no electricity in the country except for a few places. Initially, people thought it must be just a minor problem, but as the time passed, it became increasingly impossible to work without an air conditioner. The electronic appliances were of no use. From cooking to cleaning, people were totally dependent on them. Soon, the news spread.

Surprisingly, there were still a few places in India where nothing seemed to have changed. These areas were green zones, which depended on the eco-friendly form of energy, the solar energy. Here people went on with their daily chores, unaffected by the crisis. And there were quite a few places where people had never seen electricity.

Schools closed down early as the authorities did not want to take risk. Small-time businesses shut down with not a single customer at sight. Hospitals had patients with most of them complaining of breathlessness. Maybe the office they worked at had little ventilation, and now without air-conditioning the situation was even worse. Police officials were working non-stop with complaints from various places as there were all sorts of crimes like rape, theft, and murders. Financial capital Mumbai was the most affected as it incurred huge loss followed by other cities and small towns.

It was late in the evening. Eight hours without electricity created a complete havoc in the country. Most of the power back-ups that had been working for hours now had given up. Slowly, India was moving towards a complete blackout.

Sid was worried for Naina and his family in Chandigarh. He called his parents to make sure they were fine. He was totally devastated. He blamed himself for getting into this mess. He had to solve this somehow.

Surely, there must be some way out, he thought.

He could not simply sit and sulk. He had to act and that too quickly. He walked around the room and kept thinking. After a few mentally exhausting hours, he came up with a solution that seemed appropriate at the moment.

Not wanting to waste time further, he took his car key and headed towards a jewellery shop. A young salesgirl welcomed him with a cheerful smile. She apologised for the heat as though it was her mistake that the power had gone.

Sid nodded.

'I am here to buy a ring,' Sid said urgently.

She returned with a range of rings. Showing a beautiful ring, 'She is really lucky to have this, sir,' said the salesgirl beaming.

It was indeed striking. Not having much time, Sid purchased the ring.

'Congratulations, sir,' said the salesgirl, handing over the ring in a neatly wrapped beautiful case.

Thanking her, Sid left the place in haste. His next stop was the hospital.

The hospital was in partial darkness with all the stocked-up generators working non-stop. It was full of people looking bewildered. Seeing the place, a ghastly whiteness spread over his face. He almost ran towards the reception and asked for Naina. The receptionist pointed towards the first floor. Lift was out of order. He hurried with much haste. He took the stairs two steps at a time and quickly reached the first floor. He moved on taking long strides towards the room that had a board with general ward written on it. Naina was taking her usual rounds. The light from the generator was much dimmer and made loud noise, causing more discomfort to the patients.

Seeing Sid, anxious Naina walked towards him. She was, of course, surprised to see him. She told him the situation the hospital was facing and that the generators would go down anytime.

Sid looked occupied in his thoughts. He had a forlorn look on his face.

'Are you listening to me?' she asked.

'Yes, of course. Look, I have something important to talk about,' said Sid.

What could be more important than this? thought Naina.

Soon, she made up her mind not to utter a word. She had never seen Sid so lost.

Something is terribly wrong, she thought.

Taking Naina by hand, Sid entered an empty storeroom eagerly.

'Sid, you look washed out,' said Naina, placing her hand on his shoulder.

'I have to confess something quite grave, Naina,' Sid said, not taking his eyes of her.

She looked at him questioningly.

'I am running out of time and will make this as brief as possible.'

He took a deep breath and said, 'In the past few days you know there have been mysterious things happening around.'

'What are you talking about?' she asked.

Sid hesitated.

'The disappearance of plastic bags, later smartphone apps, and now the power failure.'

'Yes, I know as the matter of fact everyone does.'

'Well, I am responsible for all this,' Sid said.

Naina found it difficult to understand.

'What?' she said.

'It's a long story and gets crazier as I go on,' he said.

Sid sat down on an empty container. He motioned her to sit next to him.

He briefly narrated the accident, his meeting with *Dhootji,* and his commitment to honour *Dhootji*'s three boons: the disappearance of plastic, apps, and the last one power failure.

Hearing this, she stared blankly with open mouth.

Sid did not look at her. He was bothered. He had no time to explain this further. He got up and checked his watch.

Later gathering her thoughts, Naina asked, her voice quivering, 'What now?'

'I don't know. I . . . don't know, but I trust him. Though it seemed to be wearing off every second,' he said looking at her.

'But whatever happens I want you to know that these few days I spent with you were one of the best days of my life. Once I solve this crisis, I will be back here to take you as my bride,' Sid said, suddenly going down on his knees.

He put the ring on to her finger.

Naina knelt down slowly and hugged Sid.

'You please stay here and take care of the patients. This is the safest place for now. Meanwhile, let me see what I can do,' Sid said, preparing to leave.

Naina stopped him.

'Let me come with you, Sid. The streets out there could be dangerous. And where do you think you will go?'

Sid refused.

'I will explain it to you later. I have brought this upon, so let me solve this. I think I know where the answer lies. Don't worry about me. Promise me not to leave this place till I return,' he said finally.

Naina nodded. Hugging her for the second time, Sid left the place, turning to look back at Naina for one last time. He had decided on a certain course and acted with vigour.

The evening was turning dark, and the situation turned worse. With no electricity, all means of communication were down. There was complete darkness with little illumination from alternative sources of energy. People did not know what was going on. They were frightened. Sid's elite society where people would come out of their centralised AC homes only to get into an AC car faced the heat too. Little did they know that one day they had to breathe the polluted air. The discrimination of poor and wealthy no longer existed.

By now, the people in power panicked too. They deployed more people and more experts to the electricity board. People at the board were trying to figure out as to what was wrong. They were unable to arrive at a conclusion. They had already cross-checked the normal circumstances under which the power failure took place such as faults at the power stations, problems with the transmission wires, and overload at the electric mains, but they were all just fine. They were unable to trace the source of the problem. A few main lines were still working, which puzzled them even more. The situation was different and scary at the same time. There was something more to all this, they wondered.

After coming out of the hospital, Sid called Amit and Rishabh to make sure they were all right. He made his way through the heavy traffic. On reaching the outskirts of the city, he breathed a sigh of relief. He drove non-stop. Grey clouds spread over the sky quickly. In no time, it started to drizzle. It never rained in Mumbai during October, but today was different, and everything about today was.

CHAPTER THIRTEEN

He finally made his way out of Mumbai. It took him more than three hours to reach the place where he had first met *Dhootji*. The place like the other day was quiet, dark, and gloomy except for the little light and chatter of the glow-worms and fireflies.

'Whatever happens keep calm,' he said to himself. His movements were unplanned so were his actions that followed.

Unknown to Sid, every television set came to life and so did the smartphone. But what was astonishing was the fact that the telecast was similar. All the screens showed Sid's car slowing down on a deserted road near a milestone!

He stopped the car with headlights still on. He leapt out of the car and walked slowly. His knees bent and trembled. He looked around lost. He was so tired that he could scarcely stand.

People stared at the handsome figure on the screen and wondered who he was? Why were they seeing him on the television screen? The visual presented a strange sight.

Yes! This was the very place he had met *Dhootji* for the first time.

'Oh God! Why can't everything go back to being normal?' Sid said aloud.

With an effort, he pushed the remembrance away. Maybe he regretted the day he met *Dhootji*. Frustrated, he walked towards the milestone looking unsure.

'Shit, man, this has gone too far,' he said cringing.

There was tranquillity in the place. He breathed deeply, assuring himself he would find a solution. But doubts reappeared.

Past two months had been the extremely trying period for Sid. He was going through a whole lot of mixed emotions, and that was perhaps the reason he broke down. Sitting on the milestone, he cried bitterly.

Millions of people watched Sid. His face was clearly seen on the television. People who knew him passed on this info eagerly to their family. Sid's parents and grandpa, who were watching the telecast in Chandigarh, could not believe their eyes. It was Siddu, their Siddu. *Good lord, what is going on?* They gasped and looked at each other.

Naina and Amit watched from the television hung on to a pillar in the hospital's narrow hallway. It showed Sid. Both held hands.

Rishabh and Payal along with their family watched the television screen without blinking. It was their Sid, all right.

Yash and Kamya stared at the television screen in the drawing room of Yash's condo. This was unexpected.

'What the hell is this jerk doing?' he roared, pointing towards the television screen.

Kamya remained silent.

Somewhere, Nitya and her son gaped at the television in disbelief.

The telecast continued. They could hear Sid speak to someone.

'You just can't disappear like this, *Dhootji*. You have left me in a complete mess. You had assured me everything would be all right. But nothing seems so,' Sid grunted wild with fear.

Dhootji, who is this? they wondered.

'What are you doing here?' said a stern voice suddenly.

Dhootji appeared unseen by the audience. Viewers could only hear him. The voice was dominant, firm, and clear, which demanded hearing.

'I knew I would meet you here,' said Sid, sighing with relief. At least he could see him and talk to him.

'Stop acting out, Son. I have told you earlier that my hands are tied and I cannot help you.'

The word earlier caught everyone's attention.

Sid moved towards him swiftly.

'It all began here, *Dhootji*. Let us put an end to this,' appealed Sid.

People who were listening gasped. By now, every eye was fixated on him.

They wondered, *What is it that began there?* It was growing interesting by the minute. They watched his every move.

'How do you intend to do that?' he asked.

'Please take back the three boons you gave me, *Dhootji*,' Sid said bravely, his heart already pounding.

Boons, thought the viewers.

'I was into this because of the assurance you gave me that it would do good to mankind, but now this has gone too far. Let me get on with my life,' Sid pleaded.

'Don't you think the things I have taken in return for the boons helped the humankind?'

'Sort of. Maybe the first two. But electricity? Huh . . . What have you done, *Dhootji*?'

Viewers were able to piece the puzzle in their own way. Plastic, apps, and now electricity were a part of some boon business this young man had traded with an unknown power.

'Why not? Let me see. The return for my first boon was plastic. Don't you think your country looks cleaner and greener much like the slogans you go around saying?' said *Dhootji,* smiling.

'Yes, of course, I never complained about it.'

People seemed to agree with this; they looked at each other and nodded. Viewers without company simply nodded.

'The return for my second boon was the apps in the smartphone. How about that?' asked *Dhootji.*

Shilpa and Megha, who were watching the telecast in their respective homes, shuddered at the thought. Since the disappearance of the apps, their workload had increased more than ten folds, and the company had to recruit a team of new workforce.

'That was difficult, but maybe India required an app detox to happen naturally, so I guess we could bear with that for a while,' admitted Sid.

There were discussions on the word detox. Some understood and maybe agreed half-heartedly. Others thought they would find out what it was later. What was happening right now was far more important.

'Glad you agree,' said *Dhootji*.

'Plastic was fine. Smartphone also was something I did not complain too much about, but electricity, *Dhootji*, now this is going too far,' said Sid gravely.

Dhootji was silent.

'What is done cannot be undone. The hoi polloi out there have no clue about the blackout. What purpose does this serve?' Sid asked in despair.

Not getting any response from *Dhootji*, he fell at his feet and pleaded.

Dhootji held him. Sid stiffened as he rose. The touch was hypnotic, something Sid would never forget throughout his life.

'They do, Siddharth. Trust me they do. Let me ask you something,' said the voice.

The name was Siddharth, reporters everywhere noted this down as did the people in power.

Scared that *Dhootji* might disappear again, Sid kept talking so that he could resolve the crisis.

'It is simple, Son. Everything finally boils down to one word "desire". It is the root cause of everything.'

'Please, *Dhootji*, this is not the day to go into why and wherefore of it. I mean, can't we discuss this some other time?' said Sid, clearly in no mood for a lecture.

But people watching wanted to hear, though they could not tell how this would end.

Perhaps I shouldn't hurry, Sid thought.

Ignoring him, *Dhootji* continued, 'Desire to outdo each other in terms of wealth, fame and more wealth and more fame. Poor people want to be rich. People who are rich already want power. You buy an expensive car full of luxury at a cost of more pollution for a mere reason to be noticed, to be acknowledged, and to establish a sense of identity.

'"Look, dude, I can afford to spend a moolah over a vehicle" is the message conveyed.

'In this endeavour of proving your self-worth to others and seeking their approval, you abandon your real self. As a matter of fact, it is just a moment of "wow" for a lovely visual being witnessed. But deep down, it helps you elevate your false self-esteem. The moment you understand the significance of this, you will strive to be more us and more of what you want to do for all of us.'

People watching listened in rapt attention.

'I agree with you, *Dhootji,* but every being has different needs. There is a huge chunk of population that conserves energy too, so why do you have to punish them all?'

Eco-friendly people were happy that they were mentioned. At last their efforts were recognised.

Dhootji remained unmoved. His otherwise smiling face was replaced by a face accusing of exploitation.

'I don't deny that. There are families who have been leading a simple life and passing on these values to the next generation. But exploitation, yes, it is, and that is my concern. Earth is heading towards an "extinction debt", which is far worse than any environmental disaster. To begin with, there is a huge dearth of water which is a source of nourishment to almost all the species on this planet. Tell me how will you stop the living beings I have created from becoming extinct?' *Dhootji* said, reading his thoughts.

Sid listened to *Dhootji* in horror as did the viewers.

'*Dhootji,* I know and I have heard this, and certainly, it requires immediate attention. But this is not the way to handle it. Let us discuss this. I am sure we will arrive at a positive conclusion,' Sid said, clutching his knees.

'Son, there have been meetings, discussions, forums, and so on, in the past. Did they serve the purpose?' questioned *Dhootji.*

'Maybe by spreading awareness things would change,' said Sid hopefully.

'Oh! Don't give me the awareness crap,' said *Dhootji,* visibly agitated. 'I happened to witness an awareness programme on saving trees out of curiosity, and the aftermath of the programme had paper dump used to write all sorts of slogans. Damn it, it is nothing but a mere photo opportunity. A generation that has no time for itself, you think, would sit and listen to your goddamn lecture. You are raising these slogans because of your own selfish needs not because you care for millions of other organisms. Come on, Sid, you know better,' said *Dhootji* accusingly.

The group that had conducted this awareness programme knew of the huge paper crap they had left behind and hung their head in shame.

Yes, Sid had to agree. People had their own problems and those who did not created some. So actually, no one cared. But he could not give up. With an effort, he tried to gather himself.

'But there are other ways, *Dhootji,* ways not as harsh as this,' Sid said, growing more worried and anxious as the time ticked by.

People could sense this. *Sid, don't give up,* thought the spectators.

'It is all the same. The only difference is that it involves the entire population. Human beings are of three types: one, who understand; another, who don't understand; and last one, who don't want to understand. It is easy to deal with the first two, but it is the last one that requires immediate attention and that comprises most of the population,' *Dhootji* said.

'Yes, of course, but give me some time, and I promise to devote my entire life into saving planet Earth,' Sid declared.

'We would dedicate our lives too,' loud screams were heard.

'Saving planet Earth is not just your duty but every being's collective responsibility. Siddharth, this was bound to happen one or the other day. You were just a mediator that is all. You are taking it personally because you feel you traded for the return of your happiness alone. It is not so. Such is the unashamed and blatant human greed that every viewer out there compromises planet Earth for his and his family's survival being fully aware, consciously or unconsciously, that he or she is pushing other living beings into extinction. You talk of human rights. I wonder who gave you the right to render millions of species homeless. What if they fought for their rights? Where do you stand?'

Viewers stared at the television miserably. The words were a harsh reality.

'Honestly, Son, I know you were into it for the sole reason being the welfare of your fellow men. So stop feeling guilty,' said *Dhootji* kindly.

'I beg, *Dhootji,* you have no idea what kind of a devastation this is going to bring in. Please don't be so inclement. The consequences of this will be dangerous. There are people out there who are known to take advantage of the crisis. You told me to trust you. So tell me how my country could come out of this disaster?' Sid begged.

People begged too.

Dhootji was lost in deep thought. Sid and the entire population waited for him to speak. After a few moments, he looked at Sid.

'Well, Sid, I want to put an end to all this.'

'So do I, *Dhootji.*'

'You have two options.'

'Oh, anything, *Dhootji.*'

'You have to answer a question.'

'Please go ahead.'

'Well, name one organism other than the human being that had an adversarial effect because of these three boons, and I will return everything I have taken away.'

'It is easy, of course. There are many,' Sid said as he stopped to think.

The entire country was lost in thought. They did not know how many species other than human beings existed. The engrossed listeners coming from various age groups could not come up with an answer.

Natasha forgot all that was happening around and stared at the young man on TV screen.

'Shit, man, he is sooo handsomeeeeccc . . .,' she said loudly.

Her family stared back at her.

Plastic, wondered Rishabh.

'It was used extensively by human beings. Though on certain rare occasions, he had seen cows chewing them.'

'Placing orders online, well, who else has a credit card?' Richa thought.

'Training programmes, huh fitness regime for animals? Unheard of' thought Apoorv.

'Well, among the parents, we are the only species who worry about our children, especially their wedding,' thought Mr Pillai.

'Who else other than us would want to know what was happening around the globe?' thought the eco-friendly Mr Bhat.

'Who would other than children like me want to play online games?' Kush, who was watching the telecast, asked his parents innocently.

They looked at each other.

'I don't think anyone other than human beings would require electricity. Cavemen invented fire for their safety though,' said Mr Bhat, looking at his wife.

There were discussions of all kinds. Though the question posed was simple, yet there was no answer to it. Viewers stared at each other in disbelief. Plastic, apps, or electricity had got nothing to do with anyone other than human beings.

Sid shook his head hopelessly. He could not help but smile.

'You have made your point, *Dhootji*. What is the other option?'

'Pray, he being *Bholenath* might help you.' Saying so, *Dhootji* disappeared.

CHAPTER FOURTEEN

The TV sets showed a confused Sid staring at something. Not knowing what to do, he went down on his knees. He closed his eyes. He was now in total surrender to the Almighty.

Somewhere unknown to Sid, almost all 125 crores of Indian viewers went down on their knees – some in surrender, some taking a pledge probably, and some in complete helplessness.

'God help us out of this crisis,' they said loudly.

Minutes passed by.

'Faith can move mountains,' they said.

Free of pollution, the dark sky lit up with stars, and moon was clearly visible for the first time. If day without the use of electricity could give rise to such a beautiful sight, it was time for them to take the situation under control. Everything came to a standstill. Mist began gathering, and thunder struck. There was lightning with a slight drizzle. People moved from conscious to unconscious realm. Something strange was happening. They were in a state of trance. It was in this pensive mode that every being not discriminating colour, caste breed, gender felt they were conversing with a divine force. They could hear *Dhootji's* powerful voice again, and this time it was more authoritative.

'Earth is not all about human race. In fact, it is a habitant for hoard of other beings as well. Every living being tiniest of the tiny on this planet is my creation. I bequeathed Earth with clean air, water, and food sufficient for every organism. You inhale carbon, drink slurry water, and consume synthetic food instead. Between the pleasure and perils of innovation, you have taken up almost everything that does not belong to you. With the asteroid threat from within, future of life on Earth is fairly bleak.

'Human stands distinguished from other beings for a lone reason being his intellect. The ability to create a world for his convenience knowing how destructive it can be for the other species which also dwell on this planet is being inhuman. The prolonged abuse of environment has led to the decline in ecological footprint. You have manipulated everything to suit your needs. If this continues, what you witnessed today is soon going to be a reality with the potential apocalypse waiting to happen.

'Instead of exploiting ecological niche of fellow beings, use this power to break out of the infinite loop of ever-increasing desire and consumption and stop Mother Earth from being uninhabitable.'

The powerful voice slowly drowned.

Gradually, the gathered mist melted away, and there was a complete silence. Yes, this was one occasion every human being heard it and actually wanted to work towards it. The connection between the recent developments the plastic carry bags and the smartphone apps were evident. These were necessities, and they could not do without it. The thought of losing them forever was frightening.

Come what may each one would do whatever necessary to stop Earth from being exploited and leave behind a better India for next generation. It was always witnessed that when a divine force was involved, people doubled their efforts.

In this spiritual high, the age old saying of existence of God felt true. People had heard the story of '*Akashavani*', the voice from heaven. But to actually experience it from a medium so new was amazing.

Soon, power was restored. Smartphone came to life as well. But plastic bags were seen only in the history textbooks.

People all over danced with joy with tears in their eyes. Government heaved a sigh of relief. Yes, they had to find out about Sid. They had a job for him.

After four hours of exhausting drive, Sid was back into a well-lit city. Seeing the glowing city, he knew the worst was over. His first stop was at the hospital. He reached the reception and enquired about Naina. The receptionist was taken aback. She kept staring after him.

Yes, he was the one, she thought.

Sid did not wait for her to reply; instead, he took the stairs and walked hurriedly towards the general ward. He noticed that people were staring at him. He found it strange. Soon, he spotted Naina along with Amit in the hallway. Seeing Sid she rushed towards him.

'Are you all right?' he asked.

She nodded.

'What's going on? Why are these people staring at me?' he asked.

'I am so proud of you, Sid. You did it, Sid. I knew you would. We saw you and heard him,' Naina said, hugging Sid.

'What?' Sid asked, opening his eyes widely.

'Yes, we saw you and heard *Dhootji* speak,' Amit said.

Sid was confused, so to speak.

'Oh! Sid, you were on every television set,' Naina said.

I was on television. This is completely insane, he thought.

'You heard him? The conversation was aired on television?' he asked, opening his eyes even wider.

She quickly told him about the strange reality show ever, where Sid was the only participant and a show broadcast on every channel.

It was hard to believe. *He has his own ways*, he thought.

The news had reached the corners of the hospital, and people gathered to see the hero.

Meanwhile, in the general ward, people were talking about Sid and Naina.

'You know the young man on television?' enquired a woman on bed number two, sitting up.

'Who, Siddarth?' asked her neighbour knowingly.

'Yes, my *bahu* tells me he is in the hospital.'

'Is that so? Why?'

'You know the doctor who just came for rounds,' said a patient to another.

'Dr Naina?'

'Yes.'

'She is his fiancée.'

'Oh, that is nice. She is a good doctor. How I wish I could see him,' said another as though she was ready to worship him.

Meanwhile, people had gathered in large numbers, and there was huge commotion. Sid was surrounded by people who wanted to see him, and Amit acted as a shield. Sid knew that if he stayed a little longer, the hospital would turn into a political rally. Despite being pushed by the crowd, Naina managed to call out for ward boy Ajinkya. He was smart and had an excellent presence of mind during any crisis in the hospital.

'Ajinkya, help us out of here,' said Naina, looking at the ever-increasing mob.

'Don't worry, Doctor, you are in safe hands,' he assured.

They exchanged a few words.

Ajinkya took complete charge of the situation as though God himself had bestowed this honour upon him.

He made way towards Sid and took him by hand and led the trio to a small pharmacy from where there was an emergency exit. It led to the parking lot. He signalled a guard to keep an eye on them and went in search of Sid's car parked somewhere. Soon, he drove it towards the exit.

Amit insisted that he drive, and the trio made their way home.

By now every news channel was hunting for their hero in making. They had already dug up details about him and had their people positioned in front of his apartment.

As soon as Sid, Naina, and Amit reached his apartment building, there was a huge gathering with reporters from various channels trying to get some comment from him. He was almost roughed up.

Somehow they managed to get away and entered the apartment. His phone had n number of messages from various channels.

Sid called his parents, who wanted to know the minutest details of the recent happenings.

Meanwhile, Sid's cellphone was ringing constantly with various interesting offers from different channels. His family and Naina were not spared.

Naina was chased by a channel continuously. So she decided to answer and finish it once for all. She was tongue-tied at the deals they came up with.

'Mam, we have everything sorted for you and Sid. My channel has the best deal. We offer to arrange a destination wedding covering all the expenses of travel for the invitees along with a honeymoon package to an exotic location,' said the woman with a well-trained voice.

She politely turned down the offer. Sid was busy answering another call. He put down the receiver as well and sighed.

'Hard to resist, Sid,' Naina said, laughing.

Sid spoke about another offer.

'Wait till you hear this,' Sid said after answering another phone call.

'They want me to host a show called "Divine Intervention", where *Dhootji* would personally solve people's problems.'

Everyone laughed.

There were many more. Some wanted to dramatise the whole encounter, whereas others wanted the details of their earlier meetings. However, Sid had something else in his mind.

He graciously turned down all the offers. They appreciated his need for time and left him alone after he promised to speak to them at the right time.

It was early in the morning. A tired Naina and Amit left his apartment. Sid was relieved finally he was home and alone. He switched on the television. Every channel had some kind of discussion about Sid. One of the channels showed Ajinkya proudly narrating their dangerous escapade. He explained his heroic act of saving Sid from the hospital. He made it look like he single-handedly saved a few hostages from a group of terrorists.

Sid smiled at his enthusiasm.

There was another channel that had Yash speaking about how well he knew Sid.

'I knew he was born to do great things. Last month, when he informed he wanted to quit, I did not insist that he should continue. I knew this would happen one day. We both shared a great rapport at work and outside as well,' he said proudly.

I know for sure a break-up party is on its way, thought Sid, laughing.

People would stoop to any level to get that one-minute glory. They would go to an extent of praising someone whom, maybe, they have disapproved of throughout just to gain some instant fame. He switched off the television.

He needed time to ponder, come up with a strategy, and device a plan of action. He brushed aside the latest turn of events in his life though he could spend days thinking about them.

He sat down on the couch alone with a cup of coffee. He needed to think and think clearly. People had heard *Dhootji*. They had seen him speak to him. He was the energy behind the creation of this beautiful planet. He was real though unbelievable. He carried with him the vigour so unnerving that it could change the face of earth in no time. If he did not act upon, it would be the end, maybe disastrous one like the one they had a glimpse a little earlier.

He shivered at the thought.

People knew this and would participate eagerly. All they needed was a little guidance, which he had to provide them with. But he had to act soon after all he had promised *Dhootji*.

He went on short hibernation. Days of isolation and three dozen cups of coffee, Sid devised a plan of action. He thought of it scientifically. The idea was simple and yet complex. He reviewed and rereviewed it. He tried to pose queries and answered them. Once completed, he felt a good deal of relief.

It was time he put his engineering studies into use. His grandpa always wondered why he chose banking after years of studies in the field of electronics.

He would be proud, he thought.

It was a beautiful Sunday morning. Having come up with a definite plan of action, Sid was finally at peace. He had a light breakfast and got down to work.

His phone rang. This was a call he had been waiting for a very long time.

'Good morning,' Mr Malhotra said a deep, firm voice.

'Good morning.'

'I am speaking from the prime minister's office (PMO). We wish to speak to you.'

'It would be my pleasure, sir.'

'I gather you know what this is all about?' continued the voice, cutting out the unnecessary details.

Sid liked that.

'Oh yes, of course.'

'When would it be convenient for you?'

'I need some time. I have come up with a social venture, and it will take a while to make it concrete,' Sid replied.

'Well, how long?'

'A fortnight maybe.'

'Fine. Monday 10 a.m. sharp,' said the voice.

'Yes, that would be ideal, sir. Thank you,' replied Sid, placing the receiver.

Government's involvement solved major hurdles. Now that the financial resource was taken care of, he focused on the intellectual resource. He mentally had small team comprising of three people in place – one with the idea, another with the blueprint, and one more for the implementation. Idea was his, and execution could be handled by Rishabh. He had already spoken to him and had got his approval almost immediately. Now he needed someone with a strong technical background. At some point, he considered putting his engineering skills into use. But he hardly remembered anything. He spent hours pondering over this and eventually came up with a name. Partiv, yes, it had to be him. He had been in touch over the years.

I wonder if he would like to join us, Sid thought.

He decided to call him next morning. As he retired for the night, he thought of Partiv.

CHAPTER FIFTEEN

It was nearly eleven years since Partiv had moved to the United States. His life had been an adventure since then. Initially, it was all fun. He lived in a small house with three roommates. They were from the IT sector. They hardly slept. At daytime, they went to the office, and at night, they were on conference calls with their subordinates in India. Thankfully, Partiv had a steady job. He soon moved into a small cottage in the outskirts. He had taken a huge loan to make the payment. He was fine for a couple of years. Then the country was hit by recession worst of its kind. Not being a green card holder, he was the first one to be laid off. Partiv's life turned upside down. With little money in the bank, he was jobless for more than a year. Many times he considered returning back. But getting a job in India was not easy, especially the field he belonged to. He worked in a small Indian store as a salesperson. When his parents heard this, they were furious.

'If you have to work in a shop there, you may as well come back here and lend me a hand,' his father screamed.

Partiv did not lose hope. The industry bounced back soon, and Partiv landed up with a proper job. His parents wanted him to settle down. With recession, the demand for an NRI groom had gone down drastically.

'She is our only child. We don't want her to go too far away from us. What if something goes wrong?' said Mrs Mehra with concern when Partiv's mother asked her hand for Partiv.

A few months later, they found a match for Partiv. He was married in no time and took his bride to the United States. The following year, he was a proud father of a baby girl. Twins followed a year later. With Partiv being the only earning member of the family, taking care of his wife who fell ill often and three kids became extremely difficult. The hope of getting green card someday kept him going.

As the presidents changed, the hopes rose only to fall down. He had stopped answering Sid's calls for a couple of years now. The last he had heard of him was that he was in a rehab dealing with depression. He unable to come to terms with his eldest daughter's chronic weed abuse.

Sid called Partiv the next morning. He did not pick up. Sid left a message saying it was extremely important that he speak to him.

Partiv had read the message for the tenth time. His friend was now a celebrity. He knew all about the three boons. The news was all over the net. It was unbelievable.

He was toying with the idea. *Should I call back or ignore?* He paced up and down the hall. Last couple of years had been very tiresome. He was out of the rehab but under severe medication. He was currently unemployed. His wife had started a catering business for Indian Americans. They somehow managed to meet ends. His daughter was clean for few months now.

If Sid said it is important, then it sure must be. He had known Sid since their engineering days. There was nothing to lose. *Probably he is coming over for a short trip and would want to see him,* thought Partiv.

By evening, Partiv decided to respond. After all Sid was his closest friend.

It was midnight when Sid picked up the call. It was Partiv. They exchanged niceties. Partiv spoke about his life in lengths. They discussed the recent happenings. He had known all about it.

'Yes, I read it,' he said.

Sid covered the basics: the accident, his encounter with *Dhootji,* the three boons, and finally his word to *Dhootji.*

On the other end, Partiv became emotional. He had read this in the news, but getting a first-hand info was something else. His little sobs could be heard in the still of night. Being away from one's country could make anyone weep at the thought of divine power. All he could possibly do was mutter, 'I don't believe this. How did *Dhootji* look like?' He asked like a child.

After an hour of chat, Sid explained the reason behind the call. He explained the venture and asked him to join him. He said he was backed by an unconditional support by the government for its application.

He cried even more. A new lease of life had been just offered to him. His answer was a decided 'yes'.

His voice was shaking when he agreed to do this. He thanked God. He could not wait to pack his bags. At first he thought of a sabbatical but later decided to move for good. In days' time, he had flown from the United States.

A beautiful November morning greeted Sid and his team. Cool winter breeze blew tenderly. *Life could never get better than this*, he thought.

Three men sat at a small round wooden table in the living room of Sid's apartment. They spent days discussing heavily. They were learning and improving every day. There were cups of coffee, a huge board, papers, and many more. Sid's idea was explored in different ways. Initially, they posed an array of questions with little clashes. Eventually, all the three more or less agreed upon the idea.

Partiv for the first time felt alive and happy to have trusted people by his side. He had earlier done good-paid pilot projects and liked the concept that Sid had come up with immediately.

'The idea is a winner, but acquiring support could be difficult,' suggested Rishabh rather doubtfully.

'It is all about perseverance and how much you believe in your idea. People do have to step out of their comfort zone. I strongly believe they will,' Sid said optimistically.

Rishabh gave him a sceptical look.

'Maybe, but the technical aspect of it scares me,' said Rishabh.

'I think I should be able to handle that. All I need is a team of developers and backing of a company pioneers in manufacturing the kind of system we are looking for. We should be good,' said Partiv, taking a sip of his coffee.

'If that is taken care of, then with government at our side, it should not be difficult. Once we get their nod, we can start recruiting,' said Rishabh.

They discussed endlessly and rehearsed several times.

They spent some time working on the pilot model. They modelled and remodelled, and ultimately, it was ready.

On the appointed day, Sid, Rishabh, and Partiv reached the PMO an hour before time. They were eager to meet the officials. Sid wore small collared shirt and a slim-fit blazer teamed with blue denims. His partners Rishabh and Partiv chose to be a little more formal. Sid was elated. So were his partners. They were anxious. Finally, the wait was over. They were called in. The three held hands and wished each other. They had to give their best shot and present themselves favourably, lot depended on it.

The room they were ushered to was big enough to house a huge party. It was decorated with wood and leather. *Victorian style perhaps*, thought Sid.

Ministers and advisors, all of them were seated. There were twenty of them in the room to be precise. They were introduced by a middle-aged officer. Sid in turn introduced himself along with Rishabh and Partiv. They stared at him. They had seen him on television.

He looked more handsome in reality and had an air of confidence.

Sid waited for each one to settle down, but the air of curiosity prevailed. He was everybody's focus. They had a lot of questions, but it could wait. They were anxious to hear him. After all, he was the chosen one.

CHAPTER SIXTEEN

Without waiting further, Sid put up his presentation. It was a small animated movie for easy and better understanding.

The introductory piece had a vision that stated, 'Bringing back the lost glory'. A few scenes followed that showed India once as a desirable destination both for business and for education.

As the movie progressed, there were murmurs, and a few nodded their head proudly. What followed was Sid's strategy for clean India. He paused it and began unfolding the background of his conception.

'Our project would be in three phases to save the environment. The first phase is the one we have devised right now. The focus of this project is to make India clean.'

He paused.

'Consider a city X.'

A city layout was displayed on the screen. He indicated the dustbins kept in almost all the streets.

'Either they are empty or never emptied. So it takes us back to garbage on the streets,' Sid said.

'Yes, we know,' they said.

'I have spoken of this during my campaign,' said another.

'I had come up with several awareness programmes, but they work well for a day or two,' said an elderly politician.

Sid nodded and continued.

'With the population like ours where people mostly come from a background that has no clue where their next meal is going to come from, the terms "global warming" or "depletion of ozone layer" do not ring. They don't mean anything to them. The learned ones speak, criticise, emphasise, and finally do nothing about it,' Sid said.

'And we get blamed for not doing enough,' muttered one of them.

'I agree with you. That is why our country can never be like other countries,' said another knowingly.

'Our vision is to change that perceptive. A belief that is generally held is not necessarily true. Let us replace the "never" with "try",' Sid said ignoring him.

'So what should we do?' asked the same person not liking being ignored.

There were loud murmurs again. Sid listened to them patiently.

'Every country is different. What works elsewhere does not necessarily mean it should work for us. Before we begin with the pilot model, the people whom we are dealing with needs to be observed,' Sid said, careful not to offend him.

'Last week, I along with my friends here spent some time in this city X. Talked to people there and gained some ground reality. It is like any business model just to see how it would work. We spoke to them of our objective and asked them if implemented in a way we wanted it to would they co-operate? Actually, the results were stunning. We got almost 82 per cent of them willing to join,' Sid continued.

'Which is this city you are talking of?' asked one of them.

'We zeroed in on a city in coastal Karnataka.'

'Why so?' asked the same person still irked.

'There were certain parameters to be met.'

'Like?'

'We wanted a city that was non-metro and yet cosmopolitan, area not more than say 100 km², good literacy rate, somewhere around 75 per cent with all four modes of transportation.'

'This city meets this requirement,' asked another doubtfully.

'Yes, and much more. It is an education hub which roughly has around twenty engineering colleges, seven medical colleges, and six dental colleges. It was ranked as the eighth cleanest city in India. It has also made its way into prime minister's smart cities mission.'

'I still don't get it. Why parameters? Why not simply implement in say any city?'

Sid smiled.

'Well, sir, our project is a social venture. We want this city to be *swachh* first smart later. Capturing the confidence of people is the foremost task or the project would die at the infant stage. We needed a city that would help us do this. The past week's experience helped us to understand this better. Also, lot is at stake. The success of this project depended on how well it went off in the first city. This is a pilot project, and if we are able to do it here, then taking it to the next level say another ten to twenty cities at a time would not be difficult. Of course, it is not one man's job. We have to work towards it collectively.'

'Yes, that is what we have been asking for,' said one of them helpfully.

'So we are optimistic about this city,' Sid said.

'We would want to hear about this model or project you are talking about,' asked one curiously.

'Yes, I am coming to that. Most of the countries put fine to people who break the rules.'

'Yes, that is followed in most of the countries,' observed one of them.

'Yes, we could do that,' said another.

'Yes, but how many officers are you ready to deploy for this purpose when they have rapes, theft, and many other serious crimes to be tackled?' Sid said.

This, they knew was true.

'We are always short of police force,' said one.

'So let us look at this a little differently. How about rewarding people?' he asked.

He waited to see how they responded.

'Reward?' asked one of them.

'Yes, because without community participation our project would be a ceaseless experiment.'

'How?' asked the group in unison.

'Well! At a micro level, let me talk about city X. It generates tons of wet and recyclable waste every day. And how is all this disposed? We have a person in our building who collects the waste and disposes it into the area's dumping yard. This is later on collected by the city's municipality, which moves this waste into another area far away from the city. Here the ragpickers actually do the sorting of recyclables. They go to the dumping yard looking for aluminium cans, bakeware, tin cans, cardboard, paper, glass, batteries, bulbs, and electronics and sell it to a waste collector for a good amount. If we are still able to breathe fresh air despite of all this garbage, it is because of these people.'

'Well, that is what they do for their livelihood,' said one.

'Yes, also we have many waste management companies that have mushroomed in the recent years,' said another.

'Of course, they add on to this process and are successful too,' Sid said.

'Yes, and we have given them various benefits on tax, electricity, and excise duty,' told another softly.

'Exactly. What if we could give these benefits to every one?' asked Sid.

The murmurs were back.

'What do you mean by everyone?' asked one, though the question was in everyone's mind.

'Instead of a few companies getting the benefits, if we could make this a mass movement and bring in every individual's participation, our job would be done in less than a year.'

'All right, I get it, but how do we do that?' asked one, looking sceptical.

'Well, for past few days, I along with my friends here have worked at a concept called "The smart bins",' said Sid, looking around.

There was a complete silence out of curiosity.

Sid pointed at Partiv, asking him to continue stepping back. All of them turned their attention to him.

A counter similar to ATM counter with various chambers was displayed on the screen.

'This is how a smart bin would look like,' Partiv said.

'I think something similar is already there in a few countries,' said one of them.

'Yes, but our smart bins work differently. They are like ATM counters. But in reality, they are more like a garbage-dumping counter. The difference being that the ATM counters allow you to make a bank transaction, whereas here we reward a person for dumping recyclable wastes. Smart bins would solve a wide array of issues,' Partiv said.

After a pause, one of them asked, 'How does this work?'

'Well, if a person wants to discard the recyclables, all he has to do is wrap the recyclables neatly and place it on the metallic surface here (pointing at the pic). The smart bin has built in sensors that scan for the presence of reusable items in the bag being placed. If it is above 75 per cent, then it is weighed and points are added up in his account, and later metallic surface opens up and waste is taken inside a short tunnel and transferred into a dumping area. This is later collected by the municipality and is sold directly to waste-buying companies.'

'What happens if they are not recyclables?' asked one of them with utmost curiosity.

'Yes, we have taken care of that. If it contains say wet waste, then system beeps and the person has to take the disposable back with him. If the content of recyclables is below 10 per cent, then the card would be blocked for a month and the person will not be able use it for the next thirty days,' said Partiv, pointing at the picture and explaining in detail.

They listened closely, absorbing every detail.

'This is a great way to eliminate sorting all together. The fear of these toxic wastes getting into the landfills would cease, and we will able to ensure at least 75 per cent of recycling happening. And with rewards people will not wait for a garbage collector to collect e-wastes. They will want to do this themselves,' Partiv said.

'Yes, that would certainly bring in community participation,' said one of them.

'What are these rewards?' asked another.

'Yes, incorporating this was the worrisome part. We spent days discussing this and have come up with this scheme.'

'Well, go ahead.'

'We call these rewards as earthy smiles. In big cities, people normally live in apartments where they have a garbage collector who comes to the doorstep to collect garbage. But in small cities and towns, people live in independent homes where garbage is mostly collected and thrown by a family member or a domestic help. Most of the time, they either throw it just outside their home far enough not reach their eyes or sometimes on the roadside. We have to somehow stop the present unplanned open dumping of waste. Hence, the smart bin is one way of luring them to dump in the counter,' Partiv said.

'How would you know who is dumping the garbage?' asked one of them.

'That is an interesting question. We have designed a system that allows the user to key the card number and password. The person's account gets credited with the earthy smiles depending upon the weight of recyclables,' Partiv said.

'What is the use of this . . . huh . . . what is that . . . earthy smiles?' said an elderly looking man.

'Oh! Come on, don't you have a credit card. They give you points all the time. I mean, the time you shop with the ones they have a tie up with,' said a young politician in a chatty voice eager to help.

'I normally fly for my personal work by redeeming the points,' said another.

'Great. That is the idea.' Sid said, taking over from Partiv and happy at the positive response.

'Oh, OK. I know that. But who will go distributing cards?' said the elderly man, clearly annoyed.

'Oh, please not another card. We already have so many, and we are tired of it,' said one of them.

'I don't agree with this either. Is Aadhar Card not enough that we start with another?' pointed out one of them.

The group agreed.

'I know all of that. The card number I am talking of is the Aadhar Card! Instead of creating a new system, we thought why not use the existing one. We would create a system that would link with the Aadhar Card database and access only the information necessary for data verification and will not touch the sensitive data. This will save us a lot of time and data duplication. Hence, our earthy smile system would be an extension of the Aadhar Card database,' Sid pointed out.

'But why Aadhar Card?' asked one of them.

'Because this is one which is given to everyone irrespective of age and income. It can be done easily as well.'

There were more murmurs.

'But there are millions who have to still get their Aadhar Card done,' said a person, raising a similar concern.

'Sure, there are, and this would only amplify the procedure,' said Sid.

Most of them agreed, while some were a little apprehensive about it.

'OK, say I have an Aadhar Card. I use it while I discard waste and I am rewarded for the same, then what? I mean what is the use?' said one of them.

'Of course, these points are useful. They may be later redeemed at any shop owned by the government for purchase of food and cloths and travel by train, and they may also donate it to our NGO.'

'Sounds enjoyable. My wife makes me shop only to get those points in exchange for a gift. Can you believe that? I mean, this could do the same,' said the young politician filled with excitement.

'Exactly. Later, we may go a step further and let them redeem it against say electricity bill, telephone bill, or even incur tax benefits. After all, they are doing their bit to save the planet, and let our country be the first to do so,' said Sid.

'Yes, that would definitely bring in people to participate,' said one of them.

'Right. We want this whole process to be enjoyable and made available to all. Our mission says, "Do your bit to save planet Earth." By dumping garbage in an appropriate place, you not only make your surroundings clean but also able to keep a check on your contribution towards saving the planet via earthy smiles you have gathered. It would be easier for the municipality to use waste productively. Educational institutes could do their bit by encouraging young children to participate and declare a child with maximum earthy smiles as a "Young Environmentalist" since children are entitled to have an Aadhar Card. This would guarantee active participation from young members. It is better than an awareness program that is unidirectional. We also plan to launch a web site where people may login and check their earthy smiles anytime. We want conversations like "How much of earthy smile points have you gathered?" to happen,' Sid said.

'But don't you think having web site and checking points online again brings us back to the question of global warming?'

'Yes, so we have planned to allow a person to check earthy smiles once a month. Later, the account would be locked and will allow him to do so again the following month. And also our entire system would be solar-powered as the chosen city has abundant solar radiation.'

'I think it is a great idea. Littering and throwing of garbage on roads can be completely eliminated with less carbon footprints,' said one of them.

Soon, others joined in complimenting Sid and his team. They looked at him with praise and wonder.

They agreed upon the concept, especially the rewarding part. They were optimistic that it would bring in people if they would get something in return. Sid explained the implementation plans in great detail. They discussed heavily on the company that would be suitable to build the machine. They finalised on bringing in tenders from various companies. They decided to divert funds that were allocated for saving environment and bankroll this whole process.

'When can we start?' asked one an young politicain enthusiastically.

Sid informed them that they were more or less ready with the smart bin hardware and software architecture. They needed to recruit people.

'I need one of you to be a part of my team,' Sid said.

Almost all hands went up in unison, including the young and the elderly politician.

Sid chose the former. He was Ganesh Prabhu, a minister from south.

There was a huge applause. He appeared gently surprised for being chosen. He folded his hands in *Namaste* (a form of greeting) by bringing his palms together.

'I need some time before the actual execution. Let us try with this city and then slowly spread our wings further. All I want from you is help in setting up this in the chosen city and take care of the initial expenses. Later, my project will be able to fund itself,' continued Sid.

At the end of it, they could not help but like Sid for some reason, maybe selflessness and love for the country showed while he spoke. No wonder he was the chosen one.

'I must have a reply without further delay,' said Sid.

They discussed, and it was decided that since the Government of India had issued various rules, regulations, policies, and procedures regarding procurement of services, Ganeshji along with the financial advisor would look into the matters relating to budgeting, financial, and accounting along with all the proposals they would receive. The tender notice would be soon put up for the award of contract for the supply of these machines. They would later prepare an estimate and hand over to the board that would look into the matter of allocation of funds and also monitor the expenses. Once they get a go-ahead signal from Partiv and his team, the manufacturing process would begin.

They agreed.

'I think we should vote. It is just a formality though,' said one of them.

After the vote was taken, the meeting ended. They agreed unanimously. Some had certain reservations, but they could sort that out later. But now Sid was no less than a child of God. They would not dare go against his wishes. The meeting ended with a loud cheer of appreciation for Sid and his team.

Once out of the conference room, the elderly politician walked towards Sid eagerly. He looked a little upset that he was not selected. He questioned Sid about the same.

'Sir, no offence. It is just that Ganeshji seemed to believe in me right from the start. As you know, I have a task of convincing crores of Indians. It's huge. Maybe I would spend rest of my life doing so. But if my team member itself does not have faith in me, then the venture is a failure from the start.'

The elderly politician nodded and smiled. He shook hands and said, 'You can count on me too.'

Sid smiled. Everything happened exactly as had been expected. *Well begun is half done,* thought Sid.

This felt much better than any deal Sid had cracked earlier. The mission of convincing was successful, and the trio had a long way to go. It was a small step, but not an insignificant one. The difference was that the work no longer felt stressful.

CHAPTER SEVENTEEN

The months that followed were extremely hectic. Government had received many tenders. Finally, it was awarded to one company who were forerunners in the field. Having worked with them overseas, Partiv gave his approval instantly. When chosen city was declared, the locals were extremely happy. They welcomed the good news most joyfully. It was also the hometown of Ganeshji. He took extraordinary interest in seeing that this project was successful. His sincerity was obvious.

Sid set up a small office space in the city. It was Ganeshji's ancestral home. It was in the middle of the city and had been locked up for some time. Ganeshji was keen that Sid and his team take up this place for the project. It was a huge-tiled house with a beautiful coconut orchard surrounding it. Sid and his team loved the place almost immediately. In a couple of days, the place was cleaned up. Ganeshji had the office furniture brought in. In no time, a cook and a help were appointed. Sid and his team got down to work. The much-needed paperwork was completely taken care of by Ganeshji.

They were fortunate to secure his support. He took care of almost everything. Their first job was to recruit.

Their dream team comprised of thirty young and highly motivated people very much like iron galvanised with zinc. The trio had interviewed all of them personally. They discussed the terms of the employees. First ten out of thirty were young men who had given their civil services exams and had a fair knowledge of what they were getting into. They would work under Sid. Another ten were engineers who were employed to work under Partiv. They would be a part of smart bin development team. The actual development, of course, was given to a well-known company who was specialised in manufacture of this kind of machinery. Partiv and his team would oversee the development process. Another ten were from operations and management who would work under Rishabh. This team was a nice blend of freshers and highly experienced. They were paid handsomely.

On the appointed day, the thirty new recruits along with the trio assembled in huge room of their new office. Sid could see the eagerness to work in each one of them. Of course, they knew Sid. They had seen him. Now they had got the opportunity of lifetime to work with him. Sid addressed them and spoke of their responsibilities. His past experience came handy. He knew that motivation was the key to the success of any venture.

'This project is first of its kind, and its success is completely dependent on how well we as a team performed. Next three days we would be conducting a simple workshop to ensure everything progresses smoothly. Any questions anytime please feel free to ask,' Sid said.

All of them nodded.

The three-day workshop went on smoothly with each one understanding their responsibilities better. After its conclusion, Sid and his team conducted workshops at educational institutes, town hall, and various other gatherings. They even went door to door spreading awareness and the importance of cleanliness, but this time it was not just a lecture. They spoke of application and how they would be a part of it and benefit from it at the same time. The earthy smiles brought a lot of smiles on the people's face. Everywhere Sid went the streets were thronged with spectators. People knew Sid, and his status was escalated as that of a deity. Everything Sid said made its way to the front page of the local newspaper and third page of the national newspaper. Local television channels accompanied Sid on every occasion. This helped them to move further faster. Reviews written so far were in favour of Sid.

He took their feedback as it was necessary for improvement. The city had never received this kind of attention from the media and was keen to back Sid in his venture to make their city *Swachh* and smart.

The entire city was divided into ten sectors, and each one from Rishabh's team was in charge of a particular area. Their primary focus was to identify an appropriate place where the system could be installed. The factors to be considered were the population of the area and accessibility. Later on, they would have to supervise it daily, which included machine maintenance and garbage collection by the city municipality.

Sid kept tab of the latest happenings via daily reports to ensure that everything was advancing smoothly.

In a few months, the first and much-awaited smart bin was developed. Partiv and his team conducted several extensive tests and dry runs. Following a successful run, it was placed in the public place. Advertisements of this venture were released to generate people's interest. The earthy smile app was made available on the play store just before the D-Day, which would assist them locate the nearest smart bin counter and help them view their current earthy smiles. By the end of the day, the number of downloads reached almost 25k.

Sid's family along with Naina's arrived to the port city a day before. They were received kindly by Ganeshji's secretary at the airport. He had taken care of all the arrangements, including their stay and a day of sightseeing. They reached their hotel, and after freshening up, they met Sid. He was extremely busy but happy that they would be there alongside him on the D-Day. Naina decided to assist Sid and accompanied him. The rest of the family went about seeing the beautiful city.

They had come to this town for the first time. They had read about the place. But they were awestruck when they saw it in reality. The place had grove of coconut and palm trees almost everywhere. European influences, especially the Portuguese, could be seen in wonderful churches, which were no less than an architectural marvel.

It was late in the night when Sid completed his work. He dropped Naina back at the hotel and checked upon the others. Later, he drove back home to get some much-needed rest.

A beautiful, bright breezy spring morning greeted Sid. Finally, the day had arrived. He looked out of the window and enjoyed a strip of morning sun. The air was warm and smelt autumnal. It was an important day. Sid felt like he was opening a showroom and was waiting for the customers to walk in.

What if the turnout was low? What if the machine failed? What if the concept of earthy points went on to be a futile exercise? What if it was unsuccessful to generate the required enthusiasm?

There were many what ifs? They could wait.

The smart bin was to be inaugurated by the head of the country with Sid and his team by his side. He would be the chief guest. Partiv had taken the job of explaining the entire procedure to him. Rishabh and Sid were supposed to escort him to the venue. They had spoken to him once, but this was the first time they would actually see him. They were nervous but pleasantly delighted.

The flight arrived at the airport exactly at 8 a.m. Sid and his team were there along with Ganeshji. He was given a traditional welcome, with the playing of trumpets and drums. Later, Sid and his team were introduced to him. He had seen him virtually earlier just like everyone else on television.

'I am glad to have finally met you,' he said with a smile.

'Pleasure is all mine, sir,' replied Sid, shaking hands.

He was charmed by his simplicity and modesty. Sid spoke about how he was confident about the venture and absolute support from Ganeshji.

Ganeshji was pleased. All the arrangements were taken care of by him. It was defining moment for him in his whole career. He wanted it to be perfect. He had allotted separate area for the media who had planned to cover the entire event. They were already there.

All attention was on this city and Sid's team. It was aired on every channel.

The chief guest inaugurated the 'smart bin' and laid down the first pack of recyclables, which he had brought all the way from Delhi. It contained a few pieces of plastic and metals. He keyed in his Aadhar Card number and the password. The pack was weighed. It was around 500 grams. His account was the first to be credited with the earthy points. People gathered there cheered, and the town was in a mode of festivity. He walked to the small makeshift stage and spoke to the people. It was short but a speech that left behind a huge impact on people. It was among one of the highest hits online.

'Friends, today is a proud moment for us. Not only have we successfully implemented "smart bins" but rewarding one is a huge step. India is a country known for its divinity, and time and again, it has proved its existence in some way, and this time in the form of a young man named Siddarth,' he said looking at Sid.

'You may look at him as a boy who has conversed with the divine, but for me, he is an excellent example of what each one of us here is capable of. He represents us. My government will do whatever it takes to lend a hand to this young man. He is our guide, and under his leadership, it is our responsibility to carry this mission forward and make India the cleanest country in the world.' He concluded amidst a huge applause.

Sid's family and friends who were present and those who watched him on television cheered for him. He congratulated Sid and his team and left wishing them his best.

For the first time, Sid noticed the sea of people gathered. The road towards the smart bin was lined with people. They queued up to use this service and were curious to notice the change in the account balance. Many having arrived, Sid was free from anxiety. They would load the recyclables and check their points almost immediately. Data traffic was huge. *Of course, higher the data traffic, cleaner the city!* thought Sid.

With the system being solar-powered, it hardly mattered.

The discussions of 'how much are your earthy smiles?' had already begun. By the end of the evening, they had given away almost 2,500,000 earthy points with the ratio of five points per kg. The collected 500 tons of waste was sent to the recycling plant. They had reached their estimate.

Sid moved away. He watched people from distance. It was hard not to notice the smiles on their face, especially the younger lot when they checked their earthy smiles. This was perhaps the only country where people appreciated even a smallest thing offered to them and country were people smiled through their eyes with innocence coming in the form of tears.

Enthusiasm of the people along with their willingness to be a part of this project brought out a huge smile of satisfaction on Sid's face. Of course, the mission went on to be extremely successful. People from other towns were looking forward for this to happen in their cities too. Soon, they had an enormous task of implementing in the other cities.

A sumptuous dinner party was arranged by Ganeshji for Sid, his team, and his family by the sea. Sid and his team walked in at 7.30 in the evening. It was time for celebration. Sid was dressed semi-formally as was each one in his team. The others along with Naina arrived a little later. Naina wore a bold bright pink khadi Jamdani sari with a beige hand-printed blouse. She wore a light but deeply traditional jewellery. As she entered, she looked around for Sid. He had never seen her in a sari earlier, but when he did, he could not take his eyes of her. He went forward and greeted her. They sat down.

Ganeshji took the centre stage and went about congratulating the team for their remarkable effort. He was a weighty speaker. He spoke in length about Sid and his team. It was Sid's turn now. He slowly walked towards Ganeshji, who handed him the mike.

He cleared his throat and looked at his parents and grandpa lovingly.

'I want to thank all of you for being there for me. I must say I have the best parents and Grandpa in the world. They have always been there for me,' Sid said eloquently.

His parents had tears in their eyes. Sid continued.

'I thank my friends Rishabh and Partiv, Ganeshji and the entire team for this amazing support.'

There was a loud applause. Partiv, Rishabh, and Ganeshji smiled nodding. He paused.

'Past few months, my life has changed completely. I not only got another family but also met two lovely people *Dhootji* and Naina. I owe this success to all of you.'

Naina, Amit, and their parents beamed with pride.

'I have been living in this incredible place for more than three months now and have grown to fall in love with just everything about it. People here are warm and loving. I feel so much at home. This success is theirs.'

Another round of applause came, this time joined by the waiters and the locals.

'With my parents' permission and of course Naina, I would love to get married here,' he said, smiling.

Naina stared at him, rolling her eyes. Rishabh and Payal cheered loudly.

'I am already planning the wedding,' whispered Payal to Naina.

Naina blushed.

Sid's mom almost had an attack. *A wedding, her Siddu's wedding. God, there is so much to be done,* she thought. His father and grandpa signalled a thumbs up, while others applauded.

'Coming back to our mission, guys, let us collectively make India the cleanest country on planet Earth,' he said loudly.

As Sid signed off, the crowd gathered and cheered him to the echo. Sid breathed a prayer of thanks.

Food was meticulously prepared. It was an elaborate seafood, which complemented the backdrop perfectly. They could smell the amazing aroma of cooked seafood. Old coastal dishes with Konkan spice which any seafood lover would love to savour was served.

Sid's parents were discussing the wedding details with Naina's parents. The Singhs were bonding with the Patels. Sid and Naina sat down gazing the sea. He had many success parties earlier, but none could match this. It was way too special to be surrounded by people he cared about. He felt a pleasant calmness around.

Light sea breeze blew in his direction. It was colder than usual. The smell of the sea made him want to take a walk by the beach. He looked at the sea. It stretched towards the west. He remembered the day he had taken a walk by the Queen's Necklace in Mumbai. It was the same Arabian Sea. It had witnessed everything.

How things change, he thought.

He took Naina by arm and made his way towards the beach. They held hands and walked slowly. It was delightful to hear the sound of the sea. It was dark, and moon shone brightly. The sky blazed with stars. The sea looked like sheaths of silver.

'I am so proud of you, Sid,' Naina said softly.

'I wouldn't be able to do this if it hadn't been for you,' he said, kissing her hand.

The waves gathered at their feet. Brilliant white sand trickled through their feet. Sid stopped suddenly. He held her and looked into her deep brown eyes.

'You did not answer my question earlier,' he said.

'What?'

'Our wedding, of course.'

'What do you think?'

'I expect a "Yes",' he said, drawing her closer.

'Right.'

'I have never been so happy.'

'Me too.'

He cupped her face in his hands and kissed her passionately.

CHAPTER EIGHTEEN

Sid was adamant on the way his wedding should take place. He wanted to keep it simple and eco-friendly, much to his mother's annoyance.

'You are my only son, Sid. No crackers, huge guest list, or a lavish menu. What kind of a wedding is this? Look at the Sharma's, they have spent a fortune for their son's wedding,' his mother said accusingly.

'Oh, come on, Mama, what after that? They are living just like everyone else. How does it matter? I am marrying Naina because I love her. I don't need to prove to the Sharma's or anyone out there that I love her and make a circus out of my wedding.'

'You never understand,' she replied solemnly.

'Mama, are you not happy that your son has got the woman of his dreams and specially the one you approve of? What else do you need? Let us call our close family and friends and have a great time sharing our happiness with them.'

Thinking of Naina lifted his mother's spirits. She stopped complaining.

'All right, Son, your happiness is mine too, but the wedding trousseau would be the one I chose,' she said smiling.

Sid nodded his head in agreement.

Sid and Naina got married in a simple and green ceremony. Naina looked beautiful in a peach pearl-panelled silk *lehanga* with a stunning V neckline selected by his mother. Sid settled for a chic red raw silk *sherwani* with a contrasting beige turban. They looked stylish and classy. His mother was beaming as was his father and grandpa.

Five years later

Sid and Naina were proud parents of a baby boy. They named him Aditya. The smart bin project was a huge success. They were busy implementing it in almost all the major cities. Their concept was appreciated globally. Later that year, Sid was invited to speak in an international forum. He was asked various questions. One of them was why he had given up his successful career in the corporate world and venture into something so different.

He smiled.

'I believe God lives in my country. My work makes sure that he never leaves,' Sid replied.

He looked up, and somewhere *Dhootji* had a smile on his face.